Exclusive Souvenir Paperback Celebrating 20 Years of Inspector Rebus

Three short stories by Ian Rankin,
plus the first chapter of
The Naming of the Dead

Produced exclusively for **The Scotsman**

THE SCOTSMAN

WRITING WORTH READING

An Orion paperback
First published in Great Britain in 2007
by Orion, Orion House, 5 Upper St Martin's Lane,
London WC2H 9EA
1 3 5 7 9 10 8 6 4 2

This paperback edition produced especially for
The Scotsman in 2007

A CIP catalogue record for this book is available
from the British Library.

ISBN 978-0-75288-781-4

Designed by Jackie Freshfield
Printed and bound in Great Britain by CPD Group

www.orionbooks.co.uk
www.ianrankin.net

Contents

BY IAN RANKIN

The Inspector Rebus series
Knots & Crosses
Hide & Seek
Tooth & Nail
(previously published as Wolfman)
Strip Jack
The Black Book
Mortal Causes
Let It Bleed
Black & Blue
The Hanging Garden
Death Is Not The End (novella)
Dead Souls
Set in Darkness
The Falls
Resurrection Men
A Question of Blood
Fleshmarket Close
The Naming of the Dead

Other novels
The Flood
Watchman
Westwind

Writing as Jack Harvey
Witch Hunt
Bleeding Hearts
Blood Hunt

Short stories
A Good Hanging and Other Stories
Beggars Banquet

Omnibus editions
Rebus: The Early Years
(Knots & Crosses, Hide & Seek, Tooth & Nail)
Rebus: The St Leonard's Years
(Strip Jack, The Black Book, Mortal Causes)
Rebus: The Lost Years
(Let It Bleed, Black & Blue, The Hanging Garden)
Rebus: Capital Crimes (Dead Souls, Set in Darkness, The Falls)

All Ian Rankin's titles are available on audio.

Ian Rankin

Born in the Kingdom of Fife in 1960, Ian Rankin graduated from the University of Edinburgh and has since been employed as grape-picker, swineherd, taxman, alcohol-researcher, hi-fi journalist and punk musician. His first Inspector Rebus novel, *Knots & Crosses*, was published in 1987 and the Rebus books have now been translated into 26 languages. Ian Rankin has been elected a Hawthornden Fellow, and is a past winner of the prestigious Chandler-Fulbright Award, as well as two CWA short-story 'Daggers' and the 1997 CWA Macallan Gold Dagger for Fiction for *Black & Blue*, which was also shortlisted for the Mystery Writers of America Edgar Award for Best Novel. Several Rebus novels have been televised on ITV, starring John Hannah and, most recently, Ken Stott as Inspector Rebus. *Dead Souls*, the tenth novel in the series, was short-listed for the CWA Gold Dagger Award in 1999. An Alumnus of the Year at Edinburgh University, he has also been awarded four honorary doctorates; from the University of Abertay, Dundee in 1999, from the University of St Andrews in 2001, in 2003 from the University of Edinburgh and in 2005 from the Open University. In 2002 Ian Rankin was awarded an OBE for services to literature. In 2004 *Resurrection Men* won the Edgar Award for Best Novel. In 2005 *Fleshmarket Close* won the Crime Thriller of the Year award at the British Book Awards. Ian is the winner of the Crime Writers' Association Diamond Dagger 2005. In 2005 he was also awarded the Grand Prix de Littérature Policière (France), the Deutsche Krimi Prize (Germany) and the Icons of Scotland award. He lives in Edinburgh with his wife and two sons. Visit his website at www.ianrankin.net.

Introduction

I started off life as a short-story writer. Actually, that's not strictly true. I started as a comic-book writer, drawing stick-men cartoons with speech bubbles. I was about seven or eight, and I'd fold sheets of plain paper until I had a little booklet. Then I'd draw my stick-men. They would appear in strips about football, war, and outer space . . . until it was pointed out to me that I couldn't really draw. A potentially glorious career nipped in the bud. It didn't really bother me. By now I was ten or eleven and starting to listen to music. But being an obsessive sort of kid, it wasn't enough just to listen – same as I'd never just been happy as a reader of comics. I did what any sensible person would do – started a band. Problem was, none of my friends shared my interest. It didn't help that I couldn't read music or play an instrument. I didn't need to: the music could be stored in my head, the lyrics written down. So I invented a 'bubblegum' pop group called The Amoebas, whose roster included Ian Kaput (vocals), Zed 'Killer' Macintosh (bass) and Blue Lightning (guitar). I recall the drummer had a double-barrelled name, but forget what it was. By writing lyrics for this band, I found myself writing poetry – doggerel, admittedly, but poetry all the same, in that the lyrics scanned and had a rhyme scheme. It wasn't such a leap, therefore, to write my first 'proper' poem at around the age of sixteen. The Amoebas were still around then, incidentally, but had shifted from pop to progressive rock.

The thing about my poems was, they told stories. They were about people going to places and the consequences of their actions. I think that's why I started writing short stories. I wrote several while still at school, aided by an English teacher called Mr Gillespie, who seemed to think I had 'something'. At that time, in our English class we were given topics and had to construct a weekly short story. In one instance, Mr Gillespie gave us the phrase 'Dark they were and golden-eyed'. The rest was up to us. My contribution concerned worried parents searching a busy squat for their drug-addict son. A lot of my stories were in this – ahem – vein. At home, I wrote about kids running away from their small-town existences, only to end up committing suicide in London. One longer story took place in my own school, where a poster of Mick Jagger took on devilish powers and persuaded the kids to go on a rampage. (Influenced by *Lord of the Flies*? Maybe more than a smidge. . .)

At university, I wrote poems and short stories both. My first 'proper' short story, about a shipyard closure, came second in a national competition. My next, based on a real family event, won another prize. The first story of mine to appear in a collection was 'An Afternoon'. It was about a seasoned copper patrolling a Hibs football match. (It wasn't good enough for the collections I've published, so don't bother looking.)

I like short stories. I enjoy reading other people's, as well as writing them myself. For a time, I mistakenly thought it might even be possible to make a living as a short-story writer. After all, in this jump-cut, fast-paced, bite-sized urban world, short stories offer convenience – you can start and finish one on a short bus ride or train journey. You can read one in your lunch break. It might even be possible to write one in your lunch break. Look around you. The ideas are out there. Sometimes they're close enough to touch.

Ian Rankin 2005
From the Introduction to *Beggars Banquet*

Trip Trap

AN INSPECTOR REBUS STORY

Blame it on patience.

Patience, coincidence, or fate. Whatever, Grace Gallagher came downstairs that morning and found herself sitting at the dining table with a cup of strong brown tea (there was just enough milk in the fridge for one other cup), staring at the pack of cards. She sucked cigarette smoke into her lungs, feeling her heart beat the faster for it. This cigarette she enjoyed. George did not allow her to smoke in his presence, and in his presence she was for the best part of each and every day. The smoke upset him, he said. It tasted his mouth, so that food took on a funny flavour. It irritated his nostrils, made him sneeze and cough. Made him giddy. George had written the book on hypochondria.

So the house became a no-smoking zone when George was up and about. Which was precisely why Grace relished this small moment by herself, a moment lasting from seven fifteen until seven forty-five. For the forty years of their married life, Grace had always managed to wake up thirty clear minutes before her husband. She would sit at the table with a cigarette and tea until his feet forced a creak from the bedroom floorboard on his side of the bed. That floorboard had creaked from the day they'd moved into 26 Gillan Drive, thirty-odd years ago. George had promised to fix it; now he wasn't even fit to fix himself tea and toast.

Grace finished the cigarette and stared at the pack of cards. They'd played whist and rummy the previous evening, playing for stakes of a penny a game. And she'd lost as usual. George hated losing, defeat bringing on a sulk which could last the whole of the following day, so to make her life a little easier Grace now allowed him to win, purposely throwing away useful cards, frittering her trumps. George would sometimes notice and mock her for her stupidity. But more often he just clapped his hands together after another win, his puffy fingers stroking the winnings from the table top.

Grace now found herself opening the pack, shuffling, and laying out the cards for a hand of patience, a hand which she won without effort. She shuffled again, played again, won again. This, it seemed, was her morning. She tried a third game, and again the cards fell right, until four neat piles stared back at her, black on red on black on red, all the way from king to ace. She was halfway through a fourth hand, and confident of success, when the floorboard creaked, her name was called, and the day – her real day – began. She made tea (that was the end of the milk) and toast, and took it to George in bed. He'd been to the bathroom, and slipped slowly back between the sheets.

'Leg's giving me gyp today,' he said. Grace was silent, having no new replies to add to this statement. She placed his tray on the bed and pulled open the curtains. The room was stuffy, but even in summer he didn't like the windows open. He blamed the pollution, the acid rain, the exhaust fumes. They played merry hell with his lungs, making him wheezy, breathless. Grace peered out on to the street. Across the road, houses just like hers seemed already to be wilting from the day's ordinariness. Yet inside her, despite everything, despite the sour smell of the room, the heavy breath of her unshaven husband, the slurping of tea, the grey heat of the morning, Grace could feel something extraordinary. Hadn't she won at patience? Won time and time again? Paths seemed to be opening up in front of her.

'I'll go fetch you your paper,' she said.

George Gallagher liked to study racing form. He would pore over the newspaper, sneering at the tipsters' choices, and would come up with a 'super yankee' – five horses which, should they all romp home as winners, would make them their fortune. Grace would take his betting slip to the bookie's on the High Street, would hand across the stake money – less than £1.50 per day – and would go home to listen on the radio as horse after horse failed in its mission, the tipsters' choices meantime bringing in a fair return. But George had what he called 'inside knowledge', and besides, the tipsters were all crooked, weren't they? You couldn't trust them. Grace was a bloody fool if she thought she could. Often a choice of George's would come in second or third, but despite her efforts he refused to back any horse each way. All or nothing, that's what he wanted.

'You never win big by betting that way.'

Grace's smile was like a nail file: *we never win at all.*

George wondered sometimes why it took his wife so long to fetch the paper. After all, the shop was ten minutes' walk away at most, yet Grace would usually be out of the house for the best part of an hour. But there was always the story of a neighbour met, gossip exchanged, a queue in the shop, or the paper not having arrived, entailing a longer walk to the newsagent's further down the road. . .

In fact, Grace took the newspaper to Lossie Park, where, weather permitting, she sat on one of the benches and, taking a ballpoint pen (free with a woman's magazine, refilled twice since) from her handbag, proceeded to attempt the newspaper's crossword. At first, she'd filled in the 'quick' clues, but had grown more confident with the years so that she now did the 'cryptic', often finishing it, sometimes failing for want of one or two answers, which she would ponder over the rest of the day. George, his eyes fixed on the sports pages, never noticed that she'd been busy at the crossword. He got his news, so he said, from the TV and the radio, though in fact Grace had noticed that he normally slept through the television news, and seldom listened to the radio.

If the weather was dreich, Grace would sit on a sheltered bench, where one day a year or so back she had been joined by a gentleman of similar years (which was to say, eight or nine years younger than George). He was a local, a widower, and his name was Jim Malcolm. They talked, but spent most of the time just watching the park itself, studying mothers with prams, boys with their dogs, games of football, lovers' tiffs, and, even at that early hour, the occasional drunk. Every day they met at one bench or another, seeming to happen upon one another by accident, never seeing one another at any other time of the day, or any other location, other than those truly accidental meetings in a shop or on the pavement.

And then, a few weeks back, springtime, standing in the butcher's shop, Grace had overheard the news of Jim Malcolm's death. When her turn came to be served, Grace asked for half a pound of steak mince, instead of the usual 'economy' stuff. The butcher raised an eyebrow.

'Something to celebrate, Mrs Gallagher?'

'Not really,' Grace had said quietly. That night, George had eaten the expensive mince without comment.

Today she completed the crossword in record time. It wasn't that the clues seemed easier than usual; it was more that her brain seemed to be working faster than ever before, catching that inference or this anagram. Anything, she decided, was possible on a day like this. Simply anything. The sun was appearing from behind a bank of cloud. She closed the newspaper, folded it into her bag alongside the pen, and stood up. She'd been in the park barely ten minutes. If she returned home so quickly, George might ask questions. So instead she walked a slow circuit of the playing fields, her thoughts on patience, and crosswords and creaking floorboards, and much more besides.

Blame it on Patience.

Detective Inspector John Rebus had known Dr Patience Aitken for several years, and not once during their working relationship had he been able to refuse her a favour. Patience seemed to Rebus the kind of woman his parents, if still alive, would have been trying to marry him off to, were he still single. Which, in a sense, he was, being divorced. On finding he *was* divorced, Patience had invited Rebus round to her surprisingly large house for what she had called 'dinner'. Halfway through a home-baked fruit pie, Patience had admitted to Rebus that she was wearing no underwear. Homely but smouldering: that was Patience. Who could deny such a woman a favour? Not John Rebus. And so it was that he found himself this evening standing on the doorstep of 26 Gillan Drive, and about to intrude on private grief.

Not that there was anything very private about a death, not in this part of Scotland, or in any part of Scotland come to that. Curtains twitched at neighbouring windows, people spoke in lowered voices across the divide of a garden fence, and fewer televisions than usual blared out the ubiquitous advertising jingles and even more ubiquitous game show applause.

Gillan Drive was part of an anonymous working-class district on the south-eastern outskirts of Edinburgh. The district had fallen on hard times, but there was still the smell of pride in the air. Gardens were kept tidy, the tiny lawns clipped like army haircuts, and the cars parked tight against the kerbs were old – W and X registrations predominated – but polished, showing no signs of rust. Rebus took it all in in a moment. In a neighbourhood like this, grief was for sharing. Everybody wanted their cut. Still something stopped him lifting the door knocker and letting it fall. Patience Aitken had been vague, wary, ambivalent: that was why she was asking him for a favour, and not for his professional help.

'I mean,' she had said over the telephone, 'I've been treating George Gallagher on and off – more *on* than off – for years. I think about the only complaints I've ever not known him to think he had are beri-beri and elephantiasis, and then only because you never read about them in the "Doc's Page" of the *Sunday Post*.'

Rebus smiled. GPs throughout Scotland feared their Monday morning surgeries, when people would suddenly appear in droves suffering from complaints read about the previous morning in the *Post*. No wonder people called the paper an 'institution'. . .

'And all the while,' Patience Aitken was saying, 'Grace has been by his bedside. Always patient with him, always looking after him. The woman's been an angel.'

'So what's the problem?' Rebus nursed not only the telephone, but a headache and a mug of black coffee as well. (Black coffee because he was dieting; a headache for not unconnected reasons.)

'The problem is that George fell downstairs this morning. He's dead.'

'I'm sorry to hear it.'

There was a silence at the other end of the line.

'I take it,' Rebus said, 'that you don't share my feelings.'

'George Gallagher was a cantankerous old man, grown from a bitter younger man and most probably a fairly unsociable teenager. I don't think I ever heard him utter a civil word, never mind a "please" or a "thank you".'

'Fine,' said Rebus, 'so let's celebrate his demise.'

Silence again.

Rebus sighed and rubbed his temples. 'Out with it,' he ordered.

'He's supposed to have fallen downstairs,' Patience Aitken explained. 'He did go downstairs in the afternoon, sometimes to watch racing on the telly, sometimes just to stare at a different set of walls from the bedroom. But he fell at around eleven o'clock, which is a bit early for him. . .'

'And you think he was pushed?' Rebus tried not to sound cynical.

Her reply was blunt. 'Yes, I do.'

'By this angel who's managed to put up with him all these years?'

'That's right.'

'OK, Doc, so point me to the medical evidence.'

'Well, it's a narrow staircase, pretty steep, about eleven or twelve steps, say. If you weighed around thirteen stone, and happened to slip at the top, you'd sort of be bounced off the sides as you fell, wouldn't you?'

'Perhaps.'

'And you'd try to grab hold of something to stop your fall. There's a banister on one wall. They were waiting for the council to come and fit an extra banister on the other wall.'

'So you'd reach out to grab something, fair enough.' Rebus drained the sour black coffee and studied the pile of work in his in-tray.

'Well, you'd have bruising, wouldn't you?' said Patience Aitken. 'Grazes on your elbows or knees, there'd be marks where you'd clawed at the walls.'

Rebus knew that she was surmising, but could not disagree thus far. 'Go on,' he said.

'George Gallagher only has significant marks on his head, where he hit the floor at the bottom of the stairs, breaking his neck in the process. No real bruising or grazing to the body, no marks on the wall as far as I can see.'

'So you're saying he flew from the top landing with a fair bit of momentum, and the first thing he touched was the ground?'

'That's how it looks. Unless I'm imagining it.'

'So he either jumped, or he was pushed?'

'Yes.' She paused again. 'I know it sounds tenuous, John. And Christ knows I don't want to accuse Grace of anything. . .'

Rebus picked up a ballpoint pen from beside the telephone and scrabbled on the surface of his desk until he found the back of an envelope upon which to write.

'You're only doing your job, Patience,' he said. 'Give me the address and I'll go pay my respects.'

The door of 26 Gillan Drive opened slowly, and a man peered out at Rebus, then ushered him quickly inside, laying a soft hand on his arm.

'In ye come, son. In ye come. The women are in the living-room. The kitchen's through here.' He nodded his head, then led Rebus through a narrow hallway past a closed door, from behind which came tearful sounds, towards a half-open door at the back of the house. Rebus had not even glanced at the stairs as they'd passed them, the stairs which had faced him at the open front door of the house. The kitchen door was now opened from within, and Rebus saw that seven or eight men had squeezed into the tiny back room. There were stale smells of cooking fat and soup, stew and fruit cake, but above them wafted a more recent smell: whisky.

'Here ye are, son.' Someone was handing him a tumbler with a good inch of amber liquid in it. Everyone else had just such a glass nestling in their hand. They all shuffled from one foot to another, awkward, hardly daring to speak. They had nodded at Rebus's entrance, but now gave him little heed. Glasses were replenished. Rebus noticed the Co-Op price label on the bottle.

'You've just moved into Cashman Street, haven't you?' someone was asking someone else.

'Aye, that's right. A couple of months ago. The wife used to meet Mrs Gallagher at the shops, so we thought we'd drop in.'

'See this estate, son, it was miners' rows once upon a time. It used to be that you lived here and died here. But these days there's that much coming and going. . .'

The conversation continued at the level of a murmur. Rebus was standing with his back to the sink's draining board, next to the back door. A figure appeared in front of him.

'Have another drop, son.' And the inch in his glass rose to an inch and a half. Rebus looked around him in vain, seeking out a relative of the deceased. But these men looked like neighbours, like the sons of neighbours, the male half of the community's heart. Their wives, sisters, mothers would be in the living-room with Grace Gallagher. Closed curtains blocking out any light from what was left of the day: handkerchiefs and sweet sherry. The bereaved in an armchair, with someone else perched on an arm of the chair, offering a pat of the hand and well-meant words. Rebus had seen it all, seen it as a child with his own mother, and as a young man with his father, seen it with aunts and uncles, with the parents of friends and more recently with friends themselves. He wasn't so young now. The odd contemporary was already falling victim to the Big C or an unexpected heart attack. Today was the last day of April. Two days ago, he'd gone to Fife and laid flowers on his father's grave. Whether it was an act of remembrance or of simple contrition, he couldn't have said. . .

His guide pulled him back to the present. 'Her daughter-in-law's already here. Came over from Falkirk this afternoon.'

Rebus nodded, trying to look wise. 'And the son?'

Eyes looked at him. 'Dead these past ten years. Don't you know that?'

There was suspicion now, and Rebus knew that he had either to reveal himself as a policeman, or else become more disingenuous still. These people, authentically mourning the loss of someone they had known, had taken him as a mourner too, had brought him in here to share with them, to be part of the remembering group.

'I'm just a friend of a friend,' he explained. 'They asked me to look in.'

It looked from his guide's face, however, as though an interrogation might be about to begin. But then somebody else spoke.

'Terrible crash it was. What was the name of the town again?'

'Methil. He'd been working on building a rig there.'

'That's right,' said the guide knowledgeably. 'Pay night it was. They'd been out for a few drinks, like. On their way to the dancing. Next thing. . .'

'Aye, terrible smash it was. The lad in the back seat had to have both legs taken off.'

Well, thought Rebus, I bet he didn't go to any more hops. Then he winced, trying to forgive himself for thinking such a thing. His guide saw the wince and laid the hand back on his arm.

'All right, son, all right.' And they were all looking at him again, perhaps expecting tears. Rebus was growing red in the face.

'I'll just. . .' he said, motioning towards the ceiling with his head.

'You know where it is?'

Rebus nodded. He'd seen all there was to see downstairs, and so knew the bathroom must lie upstairs, and upstairs was where he was heading. He closed the kitchen door behind him and breathed deeply. There was sweat beneath his shirt, and the headache was reasserting itself. That'll teach you, Rebus, it was saying. That'll teach you for taking a sip of whisky. That'll teach you for making cheap jokes to yourself. Take all the aspirin you like. They'll dissolve your stomach lining before they dissolve me.

Rebus called his headache two seven-letter words before beginning to climb the stairs.

He gave careful scrutiny to each stair as he climbed, and to the walls either side of each stair. The carpet itself was fairly new, with a thickish pile. The wallpaper was old, and showed a hunting scene, horse-riders and dogs with a fox panting and worried in the distance. As Patience Aitken had said, there were no scrapes or claw-marks on the paper itself. What's more, there were no loose edges of carpet. The whole thing had been tacked down with a professional's skill. Nothing for George Gallagher to trip over, no threads or untacked sections; and no smooth threadbare patches for him to slip on.

He gave special attention to where the upstairs landing met the stairs. George Gallagher probably fell from here, from this height. Further down the stairs, his chances of survival would have been much greater. Yes, it was a steep and narrow staircase all right. A trip and a tumble would certainly have caused bruising. Immediate death at the foot of the stairs would doubtless have arrested much of the bruising, the blood stilling in the veins and arteries, but bruising there would have been. The post-mortem would be specific; so far Rebus was trading on speculation, and well he knew it.

Four doors led off the landing: a large cupboard (what Rebus as a child would have called a 'press'), filled with sheets, blankets, two ancient suitcases, a black-and-white television lying on its side; a musty spare bedroom, its single bed made up ready for the visitor who never came; the bathroom, with a battery-operated razor lying on the cistern, never to be used again by its owner; and the bedroom. Nothing interested Rebus in either the spare bedroom or the bathroom, so he slipped into the main bedroom, closing the door behind him, then opening it again, since to be discovered behind a closed door would be so much more suspicious than to be found inside an open one.

The sheets, blanket and quilt had been pulled back from the bed, and three pillows had been placed on their ends against the headboard so that one person could sit up in bed. He'd seen a breakfast tray in the kitchen, still boasting the remnants of a morning meal: cups, toast crumbs on a greasy plate, an old coffee jar now holding the remains of some home-made jam. Beside the bed stood a walking-frame. Patience Aitken had said that George Gallagher usually wouldn't walk half a dozen steps without his walking-frame (a Zimmer she'd called it, but to Rebus Zimmer was the German for 'room'. . .). Of course, if Grace were helping him, he could walk without it, leaning on her the way he'd lean his weight on a stick. Rebus visualised Grace Gallagher coaxing her husband from his bed, telling him he wouldn't be needing his walking-frame, she'd help him down the stairs. He could lean on her . . .

On the bed rested a newspaper, dotted with tacky spots of jam. It was today's paper, and it was open at the racing pages. A blue pen had been used to ring some of the runners – Gypsy Pearl, Gazumpin, Lot's Wife, Castle Mallet, Blondie – five in total, enough for a super yankee. The blue pen was sitting on a bedside table, beside a glass half filled with water, some tablets (the label made out to Mr G. Gallagher), a pair of reading spectacles in their case, and a paperback cowboy novel – large print – borrowed from the local library. Rebus sat on the edge of the bed and flipped through the newspaper. His eyes came to rest on a particular page, the letters and cartoons page. At bottom right was a crossword, a completed crossword at that. The pen used to fill in the squares seemed different to that used for the racing form further on in the paper, and the hand seemed different too: more delicate, more feminine. Thin faint marks rather than the robust lines used to circle the day's favoured horses. Rebus enjoyed the occasional crossword, and, impressed to find this one completed, was more impressed to find that the answers were those to the cryptic clues rather than the quick clues most people favoured. He began to read, until at some point in his reading his brow furrowed, and he blinked a couple of times before closing the paper, folding it twice, and rolling it into his jacket pocket. A second or two's reflection later, he rose from the bed and walked slowly to the bedroom door, out on to the landing where, taking careful hold of the banister, he started downstairs.

He stood in the kitchen with his whisky, pondering the situation. Faces came and went. A man would finish his drink with a sigh or a clearing of the throat.

'Ay well,' he'd say, 'I suppose I'd better. . .' And with these words, and a bow of the head, he would move out of the kitchen, timidly opening the living-room door so as to say a few words to the widow before leaving. Rebus heard Grace Gallagher's voice, a high, wavering howl: 'Thanks for coming. It was good of you. Cheerio.'

The women came and went, too. Sandwiches appeared from somewhere and were shared out in the kitchen. Tongue, corned beef, salmon paste. White 'half-pan' bread sliced in halves. Despite his diet, Rebus ate his fill, saying nothing. Though he only half knew it, he was biding his time, not wishing to create a disturbance. He waited as the kitchen emptied. Once or twice someone had attempted to engage him in conversation, thinking they knew him from a neighbouring street or from the public bar of the local. Rebus just shook his head, the friend of a friend, and the enquiries usually ended there.

Even his guide left, again patting Rebus's arm and giving him a nod and a wink. It was a day for universal gestures, so Rebus winked back. Then, the kitchen vacant now, muggy with the smell of cheap cigarettes, whisky and body odour, Rebus rinsed out his glass and stood it end-up on the draining board. He walked into the hallway, paused, then knocked and pushed open the living-room door.

As he had suspected, Grace Gallagher, as frail-looking as he'd thought, dabbing behind her fifties-style spectacles, was seated in an armchair. On the arm of the chair sat a woman in her forties, heavy-bodied but not without presence. The other chairs were vacant. Teacups sat on a dining table, alongside an unfinished plate of sandwiches, empty sherry glasses, the bottle itself, and, curiously, a pack of playing cards, laid out as though someone had broken off halfway through a game of patience.

Opposite the television set sat another sunken armchair, looking as if it had not been sat in this whole afternoon. Rebus could guess why: the deceased's chair, the throne to his tiny kingdom. He smiled towards the two women. Grace Gallagher only half looked towards him.

'Thanks for dropping by,' she said, her voice slightly revived from earlier. 'It was good of you. Cheerio.'

'Actually, Mrs Gallagher,' said Rebus, stepping into the room, 'I'm a police officer, Detective Inspector Rebus. Dr Aitken asked me to look in.'

'Oh.' Grace Gallagher looked at him now. Pretty eyes sinking into crinkly white skin. A dab of natural colour on each cheek. Her silvery hair hadn't seen a perm in quite a while, but someone had combed it, perhaps to enable her to face the rigours of the afternoon. The daughter-in-law – or so Rebus supposed the woman on the arm of the chair to be – was rising.

'Would you like me to . . . ?'

Rebus nodded towards her. 'I don't think this'll take long. Just routine really, when there's been an accident.' He looked at Grace, then at the daughter-in-law. 'Maybe if you could go into the kitchen for five minutes or so?'

She nodded keenly, perhaps a little too keenly. Rebus hadn't seen her all evening, and so supposed she'd felt duty bound to stay cooped up in here with her mother-in-law. She seemed to relish the prospect of movement.

'I'll pop the kettle on,' she said, brushing past Rebus. He watched the door close, waited as she padded down the short hallway, listened until he heard water running, the sounds of dishes being tidied. Then he turned back to Grace Gallagher, took a deep breath, and walked over towards her, dragging a stiff-backed dining chair with him. This he sat on, only a foot or two from her. He could feel her growing uneasy. She writhed a little in the armchair, then tried to disguise the reaction by reaching for another paper hankie from a box on the floor beside her.

'This must be a very difficult time for you, Mrs Gallagher,' Rebus began. He wanted to keep things short and clear-cut. He had no evidence, had nothing to play with but a little bit of psychology and the woman's own state of mind. It might not be enough; he wasn't sure whether or not he *wanted* it to be enough. He found himself shifting on the chair. His arm touched the newspaper in his pocket. It felt like a talisman.

'Dr Aitken told me,' he continued, 'that you'd looked after your husband for quite a few years. It can't have been easy.'

'I'd be lying if I said that it was.'

Rebus tried to find the requisite amount of iron in her words. Tried but failed.

'Yes,' he said, 'I believe your husband was, well, a bit *difficult* at times.'

'I won't deny that either. He could be a real bugger when he wanted to.' She smiled, as if in memory of the fact. 'But I'll miss him. Aye, I'll miss him.'

'I'm sure you will, Mrs Gallagher.'

He looked at her, and her eyes fixed on to his, challenging him. He cleared his throat again. 'There's something I'm not absolutely sure about, concerning the accident. I wonder if maybe you can help me?'

'I can try.'

Rebus smiled his appreciation. 'It's just this,' he said. 'Eleven o'clock was a bit early for your husband to be coming downstairs. What's more, he seemed to be trying to come down without his walking-frame, which is still beside the bed.' Rebus's voice was becoming firmer, his conviction growing. 'What's more, he seems to have fallen with a fair amount of force.'

She interrupted him with a snap. 'How do you mean?'

'I mean he fell straight down the stairs. He didn't just slip and fall, or stumble and roll down them. He went flying off the top step and didn't hit anything till he hit the ground.' Her eyes were filling again. Hating himself, Rebus pressed on. 'He didn't fall, Mrs Gallagher. He was helped to the top of the stairs, and then he was helped down them with a push in the back, a pretty vigorous push at that.' His voice grew less severe, less judgmental. 'I'm not saying you meant to kill him. Maybe you just wanted him hospitalised, so you could have a rest from looking after him. Was that it?'

She was blowing her nose, her small shoulders squeezed inwards towards a brittle neck. The shoulders twitched with sobs. 'I don't know what you're talking about. You think I . . . How could you? Why would you say anything like that? No, I don't believe you. Get out of my house.' But there was no power to any of her words, no real enthusiasm for the fight. Rebus reached into his pocket and brought out the newspaper.

'I notice you do crosswords, Mrs Gallagher.'

She glanced up at him, startled by this twist in the conversation. 'What?'

He motioned with the paper. 'I like crosswords myself. That's why I was interested when I saw you'd completed today's puzzle. Very impressive. When did you do that?'

'This morning,' she said through another handkerchief. 'In the park. I always do the crossword after I've bought the paper. Then I bring it home so George can look at his horses.'

Rebus nodded, and studied the crossword again. 'You must have been preoccupied with something this morning then,' he said.

'What do you mean?'

'It's quite an easy one, really. I mean, easy for someone who does crosswords like this and finishes them. Where is it now?' Rebus seemed to be searching the grid. 'Yes,' he said. 'Nineteen across. You've got the down solutions, so that means the answer to nineteen across must be something R something P. Now, what's the clue?' He looked for it, found it. 'Here it is, Mrs Gallagher. "Perhaps deadly in part." Four letters. Something R something P. Something deadly. Or deadly in part. And you've put TRIP. 'What were you thinking about, I wonder? I mean, when you wrote that? I wonder what your mind was on?'

'But it's the right answer,' said Grace Gallagher, her face creasing in puzzlement. Rebus was shaking his head.

'No,' he said. 'I don't think so. I think the "in part" means the letters of "part" make up the word you want. The answer's TRAP, Mrs Gallagher. "Perhaps deadly in part": TRAP. Do you see? But you were thinking of something else when you filled in the answer. You were thinking about how if your husband tripped down the stairs you might be rid of him. Isn't that right, Grace?'

She was silent for a moment, the silence broken only by the ticking of the mantelpiece clock and the clank of dishes being washed in the kitchen. Then she spoke, quite calmly.

'Myra's a good lass. It was terrible when Billy died. She's been like a daughter to me ever since.' Another pause, then her eyes met Rebus's again. He was thinking of his own mother, of how old she'd be today had she lived. Much the same age as this woman in front of him. He took another deep breath, but stayed silent, waiting.

'You know, son,' she said, 'if you look after an invalid, people think you're a martyr. I was a martyr all right, but only because I put up with him for forty years.' Her eyes strayed to the empty armchair, and focused on it as though her husband were sitting there and hearing the truth for the very first time. 'He was a sweet talker back then, and he had all the right moves. None of that once Billy came along. None of that ever again.' Her voice, which had been growing softer, now began hardening again. 'They shut the pit, so he got work at the bottle factory. Then they shut that, and all he could get was part-time chalking up the winners at the bookie's. A man gets gey bitter, Inspector. But he didn't have to take it out on me, did he?' She moved her eyes from the chair to Rebus. 'Will they lock me up?' She didn't sound particularly interested in his answer.

'That's not for me to say, Grace. Juries decide that sort of thing.'

She smiled. 'I thought I'd done the crossword in record time. Trust me to get one wrong.' And she shook her head slowly, the smile falling from her face as the tears came again, and her mouth opened in a near-silent bawl.

The door swung open, the daughter-in-law entering with a tray full of crockery.

'There now,' she called. 'We can all have a nice cup of?' She saw the look on Grace Gallagher's face, and she froze.

'What have you done?' she cried accusingly. Rebus stood up.

'Mrs Gallagher,' he said to her, 'I'm afraid I've got a bit of bad news. . .'

She had known of course. The daughter-in-law had known. Not that Grace had said anything, but there had been a special bond between them. Myra's parting words to Rebus's retreating back had been a vicious 'That bugger deserved all he got!' Net curtains had twitched; faces had appeared at darkened windows. Her words had echoed along the street and up into the smoky night air.

Maybe she was right at that. Rebus couldn't judge. All he could be was fair. So why was it that he felt so guilty? So ashamed? He could have shrugged it off, could have reported back to Patience that there was no substance to her fears. Grace Gallagher had suffered; would continue to suffer. Wasn't that enough? OK, so the law demanded more, but without Rebus there was no case, was there?

He felt right, felt vindicated, and at the same time felt a complete and utter bastard. More than that, he felt as though he'd just sentenced his own mother. He stopped at a late-night store and stocked up on beer and cigarettes. As an afterthought, he bought six assorted packets of crisps and a couple of bars of chocolate. This was no time to diet. Back home, he could conduct his own post-mortem, could hold his own private wake. On his way out of the shop, he bought the final edition of the evening paper, and was reminded that this was 30 April. Tomorrow morning, before dawn, crowds of people would climb up Arthur's Seat and, at the hill's summit, would celebrate the rising of the sun and the coming of May. Some would dab their faces with dew, the old story being that it would make them more beautiful, more handsome. What exactly was it they were celebrating, all the hungover students and the druids and the curious? Rebus wasn't sure any more. Perhaps he had never known in the first place.

Later that night, much later, as he lay along his sofa, the hi-fi blaring some jazz music from the sixties, his eye caught the day's racing results on the paper's back page. Gypsy Pearl had come home first at three-to-one. In the very next race, Gazumpin had won at seven-to-two on. Two races further on, Lot's Wife had triumphed at a starting price of eight-to-one. At another meeting, Castle Mallet had won the two thirty. Two-to-one joint favourite. That left only Blondie. Rebus tried to focus his eyes, and finally found the horse, its name misprinted to read 'Bloodie'. Though three-to-one favourite, it had come home third in a field of thirteen.

Rebus stared at the misspelling, wondering what had been going through the typist's mind when he or she had made that one small but no doubt meaningful slip. . .

PLAYBACK

AN INSPECTOR REBUS STORY

It was the perfect murder.

Perfect, that is, so far as the Lothian and Borders Police were concerned. The murderer had telephoned in to confess, had then panicked and attempted to flee, only to be caught leaving the scene of the crime. End of story.

Except that now he was pleading innocence. Pleading, yelling and screaming it. And this worried Detective Inspector John Rebus, worried him all the way from his office to the four-storey tenement in Leith's trendy dockside area. The tenements here were much as they were in any working-class area of Edinburgh, except that they boasted colour-splashed roller blinds or Chinese-style bamboo affairs at their windows, and their grimy stone facades had been power-cleaned, their doors now boasting intruder-proof intercoms. A far cry from the greasy Venetian blinds and kicked-in passageways of the tenements in Easter Road or Gorgie, or even in nearby parts of Leith itself, the parts the developers were ignoring as yet.

The victim had worked as a legal secretary, this much Rebus knew. She had been twenty-four years old. Her name was Moira Bitter. Rebus smiled at that. It was a guilty smile, but at this hour of the morning any smile he could raise was something of a miracle.

He parked in front of the tenement, guided by a uniformed officer who had recognised the badly dented front bumper of Rebus's car. It was rumoured that the dent had come from knocking down too many old ladies, and who was Rebus to deny it? It was the stuff of legend and it gave him prominence in the fearful eyes of the younger recruits.

A curtain twitched in one of the ground-floor windows and Rebus caught a glimpse of an elderly lady. Every tenement, it seemed, tarted up or not, boasted its elderly lady. Living alone, with one dog or four cats for company, she was her building's eyes and ears. As Rebus entered the hallway, a door opened and the old lady stuck out her head.

'He was going to run for it,' she whispered. 'But the bobby caught him. I saw it. Is the young lass dead? Is that it?' Her lips were pursed in keen horror. Rebus smiled at her but said nothing. She would know soon enough. Already she seemed to know as much as he did himself. That was the trouble with living in a city the size of a town, a town with a village mentality.

He climbed the four flights of stairs slowly, listening all the while to the report of the constable who was leading him inexorably towards the corpse of Moira Bitter. They spoke in an undertone: stairwell walls had ears.

'The call came at about 5 a.m., sir,' explained PC MacManus. 'The caller gave his name as John MacFarlane and said he'd just murdered his girlfriend. He sounded distressed by all accounts, and I was radioed to investigate. As I arrived, a man was running down the stairs. He seemed in a state of shock.'

'Shock?'

'Sort of disorientated, sir.'

'Did he say anything?' asked Rebus.

'Yes, sir, he told me, 'Thank God you're here. Moira's dead.' I then asked him to accompany me upstairs to the flat in question, called in for assistance, and the gentleman was arrested.'

Rebus nodded. MacManus was a model of efficiency, not a word out of place, the tone just right. Everything by rote and without the interference of too much thought. He would go far as a uniformed officer, but Rebus doubted the young man would ever make CID. When they reached the fourth floor, Rebus paused for breath then walked into the flat.

The hall's pastel colour scheme extended to the living-room and bedroom. Mute colours, subtle and warming. There was nothing subtle about the blood though. The blood was copious. Moira Bitter lay sprawled across her bed, her chest a riot of colour. She was wearing apple-green pyjamas, and her hair was silky blonde. The police patho-logist was examining her head.

'She's been dead about three hours,' he informed Rebus. 'Stabbed three or four times with a small sharp instrument, which, for the sake of convenience, I'm going to term a knife. I'll examine her properly later on.'

Rebus nodded and turned to MacManus, whose face had a sickly grey tinge to it.

'Your first time?' Rebus asked. The constable nodded slowly. 'Never mind,' Rebus continued. 'You never get used to it anyway. Come on.'

He led the constable out of the room and back into the small hallway. 'This man we've arrested, what did you say his name was?'

'John MacFarlane, sir,' said the constable, taking deep breaths. 'He's the deceased's boyfriend apparently.'

'You said he seemed in a state of shock. Was there anything else you noticed?'

The constable frowned, thinking. 'Such as, sir?' he said at last.

'Blood,' said Rebus coolly. 'You can't stab someone in the heat of the moment without getting blood on you.'

MacManus said nothing. Definitely not CID material and perhaps realising it for the very first time. Rebus turned from him and entered the living-room. It was almost neurotically tidy. Magazines and newspapers in their rack beside the sofa. A chrome and glass coffee table bearing nothing more than a clean ashtray and a paperback romance. It could have come straight from an Ideal Home exhibition. No family photographs, no clutter. This was the lair of an individualist. No ties with the past, a present ransacked wholesale from Habitat and Next. There was no evidence of a struggle. No evidence of an encounter of any kind: no glasses or coffee cups. The killer had not loitered, or else had been very tidy about his business.

Rebus went into the kitchen. It, too, was tidy. Cups and plates stacked for drying beside the empty sink. On the draining-board were knives, forks, teaspoons. No murder weapon. There were spots of water in the sink and on the draining-board itself, yet the cutlery and crockery were dry. Rebus found a dishtowel hanging up behind the door and felt it. It was damp. He examined it more closely. There was a small smudge on it. Perhaps gravy or chocolate. Or blood. Someone had dried something recently, but what?

He went to the cutlery drawer and opened it. Inside, amidst the various implements was a short-bladed chopping knife with a heavy black handle. A quality knife, sharp and gleaming. The other items in the drawer were bone dry, but this chopping knife's wooden handle was damp to the touch. Rebus was in no doubt: he had found his murder weapon.

Clever of MacFarlane though to have cleaned and put away the knife. A cool and calm action. Moira Bitter had been dead three hours. The call to the police station had come an hour ago. What had MacFarlane done during the intervening two hours? Cleaned the flat? Washed and dried the dishes? Rebus looked in the kitchen's swing-bin, but found no other clues, no broken ornaments, nothing that might hint at a struggle. And if there had been no struggle, if the murderer had gained access to the tenement and to Moira Bitter's flat without forcing an entry . . . if all this were true, Moira had known her killer.

Rebus toured the rest of the flat, but found no other clues. Beside the telephone in the hall stood an answering machine. He played the tape, and heard Moira Bitter's voice.

'Hello, this is Moira. I'm out, I'm in the bath, or I'm otherwise engaged.' (A giggle.) 'Leave a message and I'll get back to you, unless you sound boring.'

There was only one message. Rebus listened to it, then wound back the tape and listened again.

'Hello, Moira, it's John. I got your message. I'm coming over. Hope you're not otherwise engaged. Love you.'

John MacFarlane: Rebus didn't doubt the identity of the

caller. Moira sounded fresh and fancy-free in her message. But did MacFarlane's response hint at jealousy? Perhaps she *had* been otherwise engaged when he'd arrived. He lost his temper, blind rage, a knife lying handy. Rebus had seen it before. Most victims knew their attackers. If that were not the case, the police wouldn't solve so many crimes. It was a blunt fact. You double-bolted your door against the psychopath with the chainsaw, only to be stabbed in the back by your lover, husband, son or neighbour.

John MacFarlane was as guilty as hell. They would find blood on his clothes, even if he'd tried cleaning it off. He had stabbed his girlfriend, then calmed down and called in to report the crime, but had grown frightened at the end and had attempted to flee.

The only question left in Rebus's mind was the why? The why and those missing two hours.

Edinburgh through the night. The occasional taxi rippling across setts and lone shadowy figures slouching home with hands in pockets, shoulders hunched. During the night hours, the sick and the old died peacefully, either at home or in some hospital ward. Two in the morning until four: the dead hours. And then some died horribly, with terror in their eyes. The taxis still rumbled past, the night people kept moving. Rebus let his car idle at traffic lights, missing the change to green, only coming to his senses as amber turned red again. Glasgow Rangers were coming to town on Saturday. There would be casual violence. Rebus felt comfortable with the thought. The worst football hooligan could probably not have stabbed with the same ferocity as Moira Bitter's killer. Rebus lowered his eyebrows. He was rousing himself to fury, keen for confrontation. Confrontation with the murderer himself.

John MacFarlane was crying as he was led into the interrogation room, where Rebus had made himself look comfortable, cigarette in one hand, coffee in the other. Rebus had expected a lot of things, but not tears.

'Would you like something to drink?' he asked. MacFarlane shook his head. He had slumped into the chair on the other side of the desk, his shoulders sagging, head bowed, and the sobs still coming from his throat. He mumbled something.

'I didn't catch that,' said Rebus.

'I said I didn't do it,' MacFarlane answered quietly. 'How could I do it? I love Moira.'

Rebus noted the present tense. He gestured towards the tape machine on the desk. 'Do you have any objections to my making a recording of this interview?' MacFarlane shook his head again. Rebus switched on the machine. He flicked ash from his cigarette onto the floor, sipped his coffee, and waited. Eventually, MacFarlane looked up. His eyes were stinging red. Rebus stared hard into those eyes, but still said nothing. MacFarlane seemed to be calming. Seemed, too, to know what was expected of him. He asked for a cigarette, was given one, and started to speak.

'I'd been out in my car. Just driving, thinking.'

Rebus interrupted him. 'What time was this?'

'Well,' said MacFarlane, 'ever since I left work, I suppose. I'm an architect. There's a competition on just now to design a new art gallery and museum complex in Stirling. Our partnership's going in for it. We were discussing ideas most of the day, you know, brainstorming.' He looked up at Rebus again, and Rebus nodded. Brainstorm: now there was an interesting word.

'And after work,' MacFarlane continued, 'I was so fired up I just felt like driving. Going over the different options and plans in my head. Working out which was strongest –'

He broke off, realising perhaps that he was talking in a rush, without thought or caution. He swallowed and inhaled some smoke. Rebus was studying MacFarlane's clothes. Expensive leather brogues, brown corduroy trousers, a thick white cotton shirt, the kind cricketers wore, open at the neck, a tailor-made tweed jacket. MacFarlane's 3-Series BMW was parked in the police garage, being searched. His pockets had been emptied, a Liberty print tie confiscated in case he had ideas about hanging himself. His brogues, too, were without their laces, these having been confiscated along with the tie. Rebus had gone through the belongings. A wallet, not exactly bulging with money but containing a fair spread of credit cards. There were more cards, too, in MacFarlane's personal organiser. Rebus flipped through the diary pages, then turned to the sections for notes and for addresses. MacFarlane seemed to lead a busy but quite normal social life.

Rebus studied him now, across the expanse of the old table. MacFarlane was well-built, handsome if you liked that sort of thing. He looked strong, but not brutish. Probably he would make the local news headlines as 'Secretary's Yuppie Killer'. Rebus stubbed out his cigarette.

'We know you did it, John. That's not in dispute. We just want to know why.'

MacFarlane's voice was brittle with emotion. 'I swear I didn't, I swear.'

'You're going to have to do better than that.' Rebus paused again. Tears were dripping onto MacFarlane's corduroys. 'Go on with your story,' he said.

MacFarlane shrugged. 'That's about it,' he said, wiping his nose with the sleeve of his shirt.

Rebus prompted him. 'You didn't stop off anywhere for petrol or a meal or anything like that?' He sounded sceptical. MacFarlane shook his head.

'No, I just drove until my head was clear. I went all the way to the Forth Road Bridge. Turned off and went into Queensferry. Got out of the car to have a look at the water. Threw a few stones in for luck.' He smiled at the irony. 'Then drove round the coast road and back into Edinburgh.'

'Nobody saw you? You didn't speak to anyone?'

'Not that I can remember.'

'And you didn't get hungry?' Rebus sounded entirely unconvinced.

'We'd had a business lunch with a client. We took him to The Eyrie. After lunch there, I seldom need to eat until the next morning.'

The Eyrie was Edinburgh's most expensive restaurant. You

didn't go there to eat, you went there to spend money. Rebus was feeling peckish himself. The canteen did a fine bacon buttie.

'When did you last see Miss Bitter alive?'

At the word 'alive', MacFarlane shivered. It took him a long time to answer. Rebus watched the tape revolving. 'Yesterday morning,' MacFarlane said at last. 'She stayed the night at my flat.'

'How long have you known her?'

'About a year. But I only started going out with her a couple of months ago.'

'Oh? And how did you know her before that?'

MacFarlane paused. 'She was Kenneth's girlfriend,' he said at last.

'Kenneth being –'

MacFarlane's cheeks reddened before he spoke. 'My best friend,' he said. 'Kenneth was my best friend. You could say I stole her from him. These things happen, don't they?'

Rebus raised an eyebrow. 'Do they?' he said. MacFarlane bowed his head again.

'Can I have a coffee?' he asked quietly. Rebus nodded, then lit another cigarette.

MacFarlane sipped the coffee, holding it in both hands like a shipwreck survivor. Rebus rubbed his nose and stretched, feeling tired. He checked his watch. Eight in the morning. What a life. He had eaten two bacon rolls and a string of rind curled across the plate in front of him. MacFarlane had refused food, but finished the first cup of coffee in two gulps and gratefully accepted a second.

'So,' Rebus said, 'you drove back into town.'

'That's right.' MacFarlane took another sip of coffee. 'I don't know why, but I decided to check my answering machine for calls.'

'You mean when you got home?'

MacFarlane shook his head. 'No, from the car. I called home from my car-phone and got the answering machine to play back any messages.'

Rebus was impressed. 'That's clever,' he said.

MacFarlane smiled again, but the smile soon vanished. 'One of the messages was from Moira,' he said. 'She wanted to see me.'

'At that hour?' MacFarlane shrugged. 'Did she say why she wanted to see you?'

'No. She sounded . . . strange.'

'Strange?'

'A bit . . . I don't know, distant maybe.'

'Did you get the feeling she was on her own when she called?'

'I've no idea.'

'Did you call her back?'

'Yes. Her answering machine was on. I left a message.'

'Would you say you're the jealous type, Mr MacFarlane?'

'What?' MacFarlane sounded surprised by the question. He seemed to give it serious thought. 'No more so than the next man,' he said at last.

'Why would anyone want to kill her?'

MacFarlane stared at the table, shaking his head slowly.

'Go on,' said Rebus, sighing, growing impatient. 'You were saying how you got her message.'

'Well, I went straight to her flat. It was late, but I knew if she was asleep I could always let myself in.'

'Oh?' Rebus was interested. 'How?'

'I had a spare key,' MacFarlane explained.

Rebus got up from his chair and walked to the far wall and back, deep in thought.

'I don't suppose,' he said, 'you've got any idea *when* Moira made that call?'

MacFarlane shook his head. 'But the machine will have logged it,' he said. Rebus was more impressed than ever. Technology was a wonderful thing. What's more, he was impressed by MacFarlane. If the man was a murderer, then he was a very good one, for he had fooled Rebus into thinking him innocent. It was crazy. There was nothing to point to him not being guilty. But all the same, a feeling was a feeling, and Rebus most definitely had a feeling.

'I want to see that machine,' he said. 'And I want to hear the message on it. I want to hear Moira's last words.'

It was interesting how the simplest cases could become so complex. There was still no doubt in the minds of those around Rebus – his superiors and those below him – that John MacFarlane was guilty of murder. They had all the proof they needed, every last bit of it circumstantial.

MacFarlane's car was clean: no bloodstained clothes stashed in the boot. There were no prints on the chopping-knife, though MacFarlane's prints were found elsewhere in the flat, not surprising given that he'd visited that night, as well as on many a previous one. No prints either on the kitchen sink and taps, though the murderer had washed a bloody knife. Rebus thought that curious. And as for motive: jealousy, a falling-out, a past indiscretion discovered. The CID had seen them all.

Murder by stabbing was confirmed and the time of death narrowed down to a quarter of an hour either side of three in the morning. MacFarlane claimed that at that time he was driving towards Edinburgh, but had no witnesses to corroborate the claim. There was no blood to be found on MacFarlane's clothing, but, as Rebus himself knew, that didn't mean the man wasn't a killer.

More interesting, however, was that MacFarlane denied making the call to the police. Yet someone – in fact, whoever murdered Moira Bitter – *had* made it. And more interesting even than this was the telephone answering machine.

Rebus went to MacFarlane's flat in Liberton to investigate. The traffic was busy coming into town, but quiet heading out. Liberton was one of Edinburgh's many anonymous middle-class districts, substantial houses, small shops, a busy thoroughfare. It looked innocuous at midnight, and was even safer by day.

What MacFarlane had termed a 'flat' comprised, in fact, the top two storeys of a vast, detached house. Rebus roamed the building, not sure if he was looking for anything in particular. He found little. MacFarlane led a rigorous and regimented life and had the home to accommodate such a lifestyle. One room had been turned into a makeshift gymnasium, with weightlifting equipment and the like. There was an office for business use, a study for private use. The main bedroom was decidedly masculine in taste, though a framed painting of a naked woman had been removed from one wall and tucked behind a chair. Rebus thought he detected Moira Bitter's influence at work.

In the wardrobe were a few pieces of her clothing and a pair of her shoes. A snapshot of her had been framed and placed on MacFarlane's bedside table. Rebus studied the photograph for a long time, then sighed and left the bedroom, closing the door after him. Who knew when John MacFarlane would see his home again?

The answering machine was in the living-room. Rebus played the tape of the previous night's calls. Moira Bitter's voice was clipped and confident, her message to the point: 'Hello.' Then a pause. 'I need to see you. Come round as soon as you get this message. Love you.'

MacFarlane had told Rebus that the display unit on the machine showed time of call. Moira's call registered at 3.50 a.m., about forty-five minutes after her death. There was room for some discrepancy, but not three-quarters of an hour's worth. Rebus scratched his chin and pondered. He played the tape again. 'Hello.' Then the pause. 'I need to see you.' He stopped the tape and played it again, this time with the volume up and his ear close to the machine. That pause was curious and the sound quality on the tape was poor. He rewound and listened to another call from the same evening. The quality was better, the voice much clearer. Then he listened to Moira again. Were these recording machines infallible? Of course not. The time displayed could have been tampered with. The recording itself could be a fake. After all, whose word did he have that this *was* the voice of Moira Bitter? Only John MacFarlane's. But John MacFarlane had been caught leaving the scene of a murder. And now Rebus was being presented with a sort of an alibi for the man. Yes, the tape could well be a fake, used by MacFarlane to substantiate his story, but stupidly not put into use until after the time of death. Still, from what Rebus had heard from Moira's own answering machine, the voice was certainly similar to her own. The lab boys could sort it out with their clever machines. One technician in particular owed him a rather large favour.

Rebus shook his head. This still wasn't making much sense. He played the tape again and again.

'Hello.' Pause. 'I need to see you.'

'Hello.' Pause. 'I need to see you.'

'Hello.' Pause. 'I need –'

And suddenly it became a little clearer in his mind. He ejected the tape and slipped it into his jacket pocket, then picked up the telephone and called the station. He asked to speak to Detective Constable Brian Holmes. The voice, when it came on the line, was tired but amused.

'Don't tell me,' Holmes said, 'let me guess. You want me to drop everything and run an errand for you.'

'You must be psychic, Brian. Two errands really. Firstly, last night's calls. Get the recording of them and search for one from John MacFarlane, claiming he'd just killed his girlfriend. Make a copy of it and wait there for me. I've got another tape for you, and I want them both taken to the lab. Warn them you're coming –'

'And tell them it's priority, I know. It's *always* priority. They'll say what they always say: give us four days.'

'Not this time,' Rebus said. 'Ask for Bill Costain and tell him Rebus is collecting on his favour. He's to shelve what he's doing. I want a result today, not next week.'

'What's the favour you're collecting on?'

'I caught him smoking dope in the lab toilets last month.'

Holmes laughed. 'The world's going to pot,' he said. Rebus groaned at the joke and put down the receiver. He needed to speak with John MacFarlane again. Not about lovers this time, but about friends.

*

Rebus rang the doorbell a third time and at last heard a voice from within.

'Jesus, hold on! I'm coming.'

The man who answered the door was tall, thin, with wire-framed glasses perched on his nose. He peered at Rebus and ran his fingers through his hair.

'Mr Thomson?' Rebus asked. 'Kenneth Thomson?'

'Yes,' said the man, 'that's right.'

Rebus flipped open his ID. 'Detective Inspector John Rebus,' he said by way of introduction. 'May I come in?'

Kenneth Thomson held open the door. 'Please do,' he said. 'Will a cheque be all right?'

'A cheque?'

'I take it you're here about the parking tickets,' said Thomson. 'I'd have got round to them eventually, believe me. It's just that I've been hellish busy, and what with one thing and another . . .'

'No, sir,' said Rebus, his smile as cold as a church pew, 'nothing to do with parking fines.'

'Oh?' Thomson pushed his glasses back up his nose and looked at Rebus. 'Then what's the problem?'

'It's about Miss Moira Bitter,' said Rebus.

'Moira? What about her?'

'She's dead, sir.'

Rebus had followed Thomson into a cluttered room overflowing with bundles of magazines and newspapers. A hi-fi sat in one corner, and covering the wall next to it were shelves filled with cassette tapes. These had an orderly look to them, as though they had been indexed, each tape's spine carrying an identifying number.

Thomson, who had been clearing a chair for Rebus to sit on, froze at the detective's words.

'Dead?' he gasped. 'How?'

'She was murdered, sir. We think John MacFarlane did it.'

'John?' Thomson's face was quizzical, then sceptical, then resigned. 'But why?'

'We don't know that yet, sir. I thought you might be able to help.'

'Of course I'll help if I can. Sit down, please.'

Rebus perched on the chair, while Thomson pushed aside some newspapers and settled himself on the sofa.

'You're a writer, I believe,' said Rebus.

Thomson nodded distractedly. 'Yes,' he said. 'Freelance journalism, food and drink, travel, that sort of thing. Plus the occasional commission to write a book. That's what I'm doing now, actually. Writing a book.'

'Oh? I like books myself. What's it about?'

'Don't laugh,' said Thomson, 'but it's a history of the haggis.'

'The haggis?' Rebus couldn't disguise a smile in his voice, warmer this time: the church pew had been given a cushion. He cleared his throat noisily, glancing around the room, noting the piles of books leaning precariously against walls, the files and folders and newsprint cuttings. 'You must do a lot of research,' he said appreciatively.

'Sometimes,' said Thomson. Then he shook his head. 'I still can't believe it. About Moira, I mean. About John.'

Rebus took out his notebook, more for effect than anything else. 'You were Miss Bitter's lover for a while,' he stated.

'That's right, Inspector.'

'But then she went off with Mr MacFarlane.'

'Right again.' A hint of bitterness had crept into Thomson's voice. 'I was very angry at the time, but I got over it.'

'Did you still see Miss Bitter?'

'No.'

'What about Mr MacFarlane?'

'No again. We spoke on the telephone a couple of times. It always seemed to end in a shouting match. We used to be like, well, it's a cliché, I suppose, but we used to be like brothers.'

'Yes,' said Rebus, 'so Mr MacFarlane told me.'

'Oh?' Thomson sounded interested. 'What else did he say?'

'Not much really.' Rebus rose from his perch and went to the window, holding aside the net curtain to stare out onto the street below. 'He said you'd known each other for years.'

'Since school,' Thomson added.

Rebus nodded. 'And he said you drove a black Ford Escort. That'll be it down there, parked across the street?'

Thomson came to the window. 'Yes,' he agreed, uncertainly, 'that's it. But I don't see what –'

'I noticed it as I was parking my own car,' Rebus continued, brushing past Thomson's interruption. He let the curtain fall and turned back into the room. 'I noticed you've got a car alarm. I suppose you must get a lot of burglaries around here.'

'It's not the most salubrious part of town,' Thomson said. 'Not all writers are like Jeffrey Archer.'

'Did money have anything to do with it?' Rebus asked. Thomson paused.

'With what, Inspector?'

'With Miss Bitter leaving you for Mr MacFarlane. He's not short of a bob or two, is he?'

Thomson's voice rose perceptibly. 'Look, I really can't see what this has to do with –'

'Your car was broken into a few months ago, wasn't it?' Rebus was examining a pile of magazines on the floor now. 'I saw the report. They stole your radio and your car phone.'

'Yes.'

'I notice you've replaced the car phone.' He glanced up at Thomson, smiled, and continued browsing.

'Of course,' said Thomson. He seemed confused now, unable to fathom where the conversation was leading.

'A journalist would need a car phone, wouldn't he?' Rebus observed. 'So people could keep in touch, contact him at any time. Is that right?'

'Absolutely right, Inspector.'

Rebus threw the magazine back onto the pile and nodded slowly. 'Great things, car phones.' He walked over towards Thomson's desk. It was a small flat. This room obviously served a double purpose as study and living-room. Not that Thomson entertained many visitors. He was too aggressive for many people, too secretive for others. So John MacFarlane had said.

On the desk there was more clutter, though in some appearance of organisation. There was also a neat word processor, and beside it a telephone. And next to the telephone sat an answering machine.

'Yes,' Rebus repeated. 'You need to be in contact.' Rebus smiled towards Thomson. 'Communication, that's the secret. And I'll tell you something else about journalists.'

'What?' Unable to comprehend Rebus's direction, Thomson's tone had become that of someone bored with a conversation. He shoved his hands deep into his pockets.

'Journalists are hoarders.' Rebus made this sound like some great wisdom. His eyes took in the room again. 'I mean, near-pathological hoarders. They can't bear to throw things away, because they never know when something might become useful. Am I right?'

Thomson shrugged.

'Yes,' said Rebus, 'I bet I am. Look at these cassettes, for example.' He went to where the rows of tapes were neatly displayed. 'What are they? Interviews, that sort of thing?'

'Mostly, yes,' Thomson agreed.

'And you still keep them, even though they're years old?'

Thomson shrugged again. 'So I'm a hoarder.'

But Rebus had noticed something on the top shelf, some brown cardboard boxes. He reached up and lifted one down. Inside were more tapes, marked with months and years. But these tapes were smaller. Rebus gestured with the box towards Thomson, his eyes seeking an explanation.

Thomson smiled uneasily. 'Answering machine messages,' he said.

'You keep these, too?' Rebus sounded amazed.

'Well,' Thomson said, 'someone may agree to something over the phone, an interview or something, then deny it later. I need them as records of promises made.'

Rebus nodded, understanding now. He replaced the brown box on its shelf. He still had his back to Thomson when the telephone rang, a sharp electronic sound.

'Sorry,' Thomson apologised, going to answer it.

'Not at all.'

Thomson picked up the receiver. 'Hello?' He listened, then

frowned. 'Of course,' he said finally, holding the receiver out towards Rebus. 'It's for you, Inspector.'

Rebus raised a surprised eyebrow and accepted the receiver. It was, as he had known it would be, Detective Constable Holmes.

'Okay,' Holmes said. 'Costain no longer owes you that favour. He's listened to both tapes. He hasn't run all the necessary tests yet, but he's pretty convinced.'

'Go on.' Rebus was looking at Thomson, who was sitting, hands clasping knees, on the arm of the chair.

'The call we received last night,' said Holmes, 'the one from John MacFarlane admitting to the murder of Moira Bitter, originated from a portable telephone.'

'Interesting,' said Rebus, his eyes on Thomson. 'And what about the other one?'

'Well, the tape you gave me seems to be twice-removed.'

'What does that mean?'

'It means,' said Holmes, 'that according to Costain it's not just a recording, it's the recording of a recording.' Rebus nodded, satisfied.

'Okay, thanks, Brian.' He put down the receiver.

'Good news or bad?' Thomson asked.

'A bit of both,' answered Rebus thoughtfully. Thomson had risen to his feet.

'I feel like a drink, Inspector. Can I get you one?'

'It's a bit early for me, I'm afraid,' Rebus said, looking at his watch. It was eleven o'clock: opening time. 'All right,' he said, 'just a small one.'

'The whisky's in the kitchen,' Thomson explained. 'I'll just be a moment.'

'Fine, sir, fine.'

Rebus listened as Thomson left the room and headed off towards the kitchen. He stood beside the desk, thinking through what he now knew. Then, hearing Thomson returning from the kitchen, floorboards bending beneath his weight, he picked up the wastepaper basket from below the desk, and, as Thomson entered the room, proceeded to empty the contents in a heap on the sofa.

Thomson stood in the doorway, a glass of whisky in each hand, dumbstruck. 'What on earth are you doing?' he spluttered at last. But Rebus ignored him and started to pick through the now strewn contents of the bin, talking as he searched.

'It was pretty close to being foolproof, Mr Thomson. Let me explain. The killer went to Moira Bitter's flat and talked her into letting him in despite the late hour. He murdered her quite callously, let's make no mistake about that. I've never seen so much premeditation in a case before. He cleaned the knife and returned it to its drawer. He was wearing gloves, of course, knowing John MacFarlane's fingerprints would be all over the flat, and he cleaned the knife precisely to disguise the fact that he *had* worn gloves. MacFarlane, you see, had not.'

Thomson took a gulp from one glass, but otherwise seemed rooted to the spot. His eyes had become vacant, as though picturing Rebus's story in his mind.

'MacFarlane,' Rebus continued, still rummaging, 'was summoned to Moira's flat. The message did come from her. He knew her voice well enough not to be fooled by someone else's voice. The killer sat outside Moira's flat, sat waiting for MacFarlane to arrive. Then the killer made one last call, this one to the police, in the guise of an hysterical MacFarlane. We know this last call was made on a car phone. The lab boys are very clever that way. The police are hoarders, too, you see, Mr Thomson. We make recordings of emergency calls made to us. It won't be hard to voice-print that call and try to match it to John MacFarlane. But it won't be John MacFarlane, will it?' Rebus paused for effect. 'It'll be you.'

Thomson gave a thin smile, but his grip on the two glasses had grown less steady, and whisky was dribbling from the angled lip of one of them.

'Ah-ha.' Rebus had found what he was looking for in the contents of the bin. With a pleased-as-Punch grin on his unshaven, sleepless face, he pinched forefinger and thumb together and lifted them for his own and Thomson's inspection. He was holding a tiny sliver of brown recording tape.

'You see,' he continued, 'the killer had to lure MacFarlane to the murder scene. Having killed Moira, he went to his car, as I've said. There he had his portable telephone and a cassette recorder. He was a hoarder. He had kept all his answering machine tapes, including messages left by Moira at the height of their affair. He found the message he needed and he spliced it. He played this message to John MacFarlane's answering machine. All he had to do after that was wait. The message MacFarlane received was "Hello. I need to see you." There was a pause after the "hello". And that pause was where the splice was made in the tape, excising this.' Rebus looked at the sliver of tape. 'The one word "Kenneth". "Hello, Kenneth, I need to see you." It was Moira Bitter talking to you, Mr Thomson, talking to you a long time ago.'

Thomson hurled both glasses at once, so that they arrowed in towards Rebus, who ducked. The glasses collided above his head, shards raining down on him. Thomson had reached the front door, had hauled it open even, before Rebus was on him, lunging, pushing the younger man forwards through the doorway and onto the tenement landing. Thomson's head hit the metal rails with a muted chime and he let out a single moan before collapsing. Rebus shook himself free of glass, feeling one or two tiny pieces nick him as he brushed a hand across his face. He brought a hand to his nose and inhaled deeply. His father had always said whisky would put hairs on his chest. Rebus wondered if the same miracle might be effected on his temples and the crown of his head . . .

It had been the perfect murder.

Well, almost. But Kenneth Thomson had reckoned without Rebus's ability actually to believe someone innocent despite the evidence against him. The case against John MacFarlane had been overwhelming. Yet Rebus, feeling it to be wrong, had been forced to invent other scenarios, other motives and other means to the fairly chilling end. It wasn't enough that

Moira had died – died at the hands of someone she knew. MacFarlane had to be implicated in her murder. The killer had been out to tag them both. But it was Moira the killer hated, hated because she had broken a friendship as well as a heart.

Rebus stood on the steps of the police station. Thomson was in a cell somewhere below his feet, somewhere below ground level. Confessing to everything. He would go to jail, while John MacFarlane, perhaps not realising his luck, had already been freed.

The streets were busy now. Lunchtime traffic, the reliable noises of the everyday. The sun was even managing to burst from its slumber. All of which reminded Rebus that his day was over. Time, all in all he felt, for a short visit home, a shower and a change of clothes, and, God and the Devil willing, some sleep.

THE DEAN CURSE

AN INSPECTOR REBUS STORY

The locals in Barnton knew him either as 'the Brigadier' or as 'that Army type who bought the West Lodge'. West Lodge was a huge but until recently neglected detached house set in a walled acre and a half of grounds and copses. Most locals were relieved that its high walls hid it from general view, the house itself being too angular, too gothic for modern tastes. Certainly, it was very large for the needs of a widower and his unsmiling daughter. Mrs MacLennan, who cleaned for the Brigadier, was pumped for information by curious neighbours, but could say only that Brigadier-General Dean had had some renovations done, that most of the house was habitable, that one room had become a library, another a billiard-room, another a study, another a makeshift gymnasium and so on. The listeners would drink this in deeply, yet it was never enough. What about the daughter? What about the Brigadier's background? What happened to his wife?

Shopkeepers too were asked for their thoughts. The Brigadier drove a sporty open-topped car which would pull in noisily to the side of the road to allow him to pop into this or that shop for a few things, including, each day at the same time, a bottle of something or other from the smarter of the two off-licences.

The grocer, Bob Sladden, reckoned that Brigadier-General Dean had been born nearby, even that he had lived for a few childhood years in West Lodge and so had retired there because of its carefree connections. But Miss Dalrymple, who at ninety-three was as old as anyone in that part of Barnton, could not recall any family named Dean living at

West Lodge. Could not, indeed, recall any Deans ever living in this 'neck' of Barnton, with the exception of Sam Dean. But when pressed about Sam Dean, she merely shook her head and said, 'He was no good, that one, and got what he deserved. The Great War saw to him.' Then she would nod slowly, thoughtfully, and nobody would be any further forward.

Speculation grew wilder as no new facts came to light, and in the Claymore public bar one afternoon, a bar never patronised by the Brigadier (and who'd ever heard of an Army man not liking his drink?), a young out-of-work plasterer named Willie Barr came up with a fresh proposition.

'Maybe Dean isn't his real name.'

But everyone around the pool table laughed at that and Willie just shrugged, readying to play his next shot. 'Well,' he said, 'real name or not, I wouldn't climb over that daughter of his to get to any of you lot.'

Then he played a double off the cushion, but missed. Missed not because the shot was difficult or he'd had too many pints of Snakebite, but because his cue arm jerked at the noise of the explosion.

It was a fancy car all right, a Jaguar XJS convertible, its bodywork a startling red. Nobody in Barnton could mistake it for anyone else's car. Besides, everyone was used to it revving to its loud roadside halt, was used to its contented ticking-over while the Brigadier did his shopping. Some complained – though never to his face – about the noise, about the fumes from the exhaust. They couldn't say why he never switched off the ignition. He always seemed to want to be ready for a quick getaway. On this particular afternoon, the getaway was quicker even than usual, a squeal of tyres as the car jerked out into the road and sped past the shops. Its driver seemed ready actually to disregard the red stop light at the busy junction. He never got the chance. There was a ball of flames where the car had been and the heart-stopping sound of the explosion. Twisted metal flew into the air, then down again, wounding passers-by, burning skin. Shop windows blew in, shards of fine glass finding soft targets. The traffic lights turned to green, but nothing moved in the street.

For a moment, there was a silence punctuated only by the arrival on terra firma of bits of speedometer, headlamp, even steering-wheel. Then the screaming started, as people realised they'd been wounded. More curdling still though were the silences, the dumb horrified faces of people who would never forget this moment, whose shock would disturb each wakeful night.

And then there was a man, standing in a doorway, the doorway of what had been the wine merchant's. He carried a bottle with him, carefully wrapped in green paper, and his mouth was open in surprise. He dropped the bottle with a crash when he realised his car was not where he had left it, realising that the roaring he had heard and thought he recognised was that of his own car being driven away. At his feet, he saw one of his driving gloves lying on the pavement in front of him. It was still smouldering. Only five minutes before, it had been lying on the leather of his passenger seat. The wine merchant was standing beside him now, pale and shaking, looking in dire need of a drink. The Brigadier nodded towards the carcass of his sleek red Jaguar.

'That should have been me,' he said. Then: 'Do you mind if I use your telephone?'

John Rebus threw *The Dain Curse* up in the air, sending it spinning towards his living-room ceiling. Gravity caught up with it just short of the ceiling and pulled it down hard, so that it landed open against the uncarpeted floor. It was a cheap copy, bought secondhand and previously much read. But not by Rebus; he'd got as far as the beginning of the third section, 'Quesada', before giving up, before tossing what many regard as Hammett's finest novel into the air. Its pages fell away from the spine as it landed, scattering chapters. Rebus growled. The telephone had, as though prompted by the book's demise, started ringing. Softly, insistently. Rebus picked up the apparatus and studied it. It was six o'clock on the evening of his first rest-day in what seemed like months. Who would be phoning him? Pleasure or business? And which would he prefer it to be? He put the receiver to his ear.

'Yes?' His voice was non-committal.

'DI Rebus?' It was work then. Rebus grunted a response. 'DC Coupar here, sir. The Chief thought you'd be interested.' There was a pause for effect. 'A bomb's just gone off in Barnton.'

Rebus stared at the sheets of print lying all around him. He asked the Detective Constable to repeat the message.

'A bomb, sir. In Barnton.'

'What? A World War Two leftover you mean?'

'No, sir. Nothing like that. Nothing like that at all.'

There was a line of poetry in Rebus's head as he drove out towards one of Edinburgh's many quiet middle-class districts, the sort of place where nothing happened, the sort of place where crime was measured in a yearly attempted break-in or the theft of a bicycle. That was Barnton. The line of poetry hadn't been written about Barnton. It had been written about Slough.

It's my own fault, Rebus was thinking, for being disgusted at how far-fetched that Hammett book was. Entertaining, yes, but you could strain credulity only so far, and Dashiell Hammett had taken that strain like the anchor-man on a tug-o'-war team, pulling with all his might. Coincidence after coincidence, plot after plot, corpse following corpse like something off an assembly line.

Far-fetched, definitely. But then what was Rebus to make of his telephone call? He'd checked: it wasn't 1st April. But then he wouldn't put it past Brian Holmes or one of his other colleagues to pull a stunt on him just because he was having a day off, just because he'd carped on about it for the previous few days. Yes, this had Holmes' fingerprints all over it. Except for one thing.

The radio reports. The police frequency was full of it; and when Rebus switched on his car radio to the local commercial channel, the news was there, too. Reports of an explosion in Barnton, not far from the roundabout. It is thought a car has exploded. No further details, though there are thought to be many casualties. Rebus shook his head and drove, thinking of the poem again, thinking of anything that would stop him focussing on the truth of the news. A car bomb? *A car bomb?* In Belfast, yes, maybe even on occasion in London. But here in Edinburgh? Rebus blamed himself. If only he hadn't cursed Dashiell Hammett, if only he hadn't sneered at his book, at its exaggerations and its melodramas, if only . . . Then none of this would have happened.

But of course it would. It had.

The road had been blocked off. The ambulances had left with their cargo. Onlookers stood four deep behind the orange and white tape of the hastily erected cordon. There was just the one question: how many dead? The answer seemed to be: just the one. The driver of the car. An Army bomb disposal unit had materialised from somewhere and, for want of anything else to do, was checking the shops either side of the street. A line of policemen, aided so far as Rebus could judge by more Army personnel, was moving slowly up the road, mostly on hands and knees, in what an outsider might regard as some bizarre slow-motion race. They carried with them polythene bags, into which they dropped anything they found. The whole scene was one of brilliantly organised confusion and it didn't take Rebus longer than a couple of minutes to detect the mastermind behind it all – Superintendent 'Farmer' Watson. 'Farmer' only behind his back, of course, and a nickname which matched both his north-of-Scotland background and his at times agricultural methods. Rebus decided to skirt around his superior officer and glean what he could from the various less senior officers present.

He had come to Barnton with a set of preconceptions and it took time for these to be corrected. For example, he'd premised that the person in the car, the as-yet-unidentified deceased, would be the car's owner and that this person would have been the target of the bomb attack (the evidence all around most certainly pointed to a bomb, rather than spontaneous combustion, say, or any other more likely explanation). Either that or the car might be stolen or borrowed, and the driver some sort of terrorist, blown apart by his own device before he could leave it at its intended destination. There were certainly Army installations around Edinburgh: barracks, armouries, listening posts. Across the Forth lay what was left of Rosyth naval dockyard, as well as the underground installation at Pitreavie. There were targets. Bomb meant terrorist meant target. That was how it always was.

But not this time. This time there was an important difference. The apparent target escaped, by dint of leaving his car for a couple of minutes to nip into a shop. But while he was in the shop someone had tried to steal his car, and that person was now drying into the tarmac beneath the knees of the crawling policemen. This much Rebus learned before Superintendent Watson caught sight of him, caught sight of him smiling wryly at the car thief's luck. It wasn't every day you got the chance to steal a Jaguar XJS . . . but what a day to pick.

'Inspector!' Farmer Watson beckoned for Rebus to join him, which Rebus, ironing out his smile, did.

Before Watson could start filling him in on what he already knew, Rebus himself spoke.

'Who was the target, sir?'

'A man called Dean.' Meaningful pause. 'Brigadier-General Dean, retired.'

Rebus nodded. 'I thought there were a lot of Tommies about.'

'We'll be working with the Army on this one, John. That's how it's done, apparently. And then there's Scotland Yard, too. Their anti-terrorist people.'

'Too many cooks if you ask me, sir.'

Watson nodded. 'Still, these buggers are supposed to be specialised.'

'And we're only good for solving the odd drunk-driving

or domestic, eh, sir?'

The two men shared a smile at this. Rebus nodded towards the wreck of the car. 'Any idea who was behind the wheel?'

Watson shook his head. 'Not yet. And not much to go on either. We may have to wait till a mum or girlfriend reports him missing.'

'Not even a description?'

'None of the passers-by is fit to be questioned. Not yet anyway.'

'So what about Brigadier-General Whassisname?'

'Dean.'

'Yes. Where is he?'

'He's at home. A doctor's been to take a look at him, but he seems all right. A bit shocked.'

'A bit? Someone rips the arse out of his car and he's a *bit* shocked?' Rebus sounded doubtful. Watson's eyes were fixed on the advancing line of debris collectors.

'I get the feeling he's seen worse.' He turned to Rebus. 'Why don't you have a word with him, John? See what you think.'

Rebus nodded slowly. 'Aye, why not,' he said. 'Anything for a laugh, eh, sir?'

Watson seemed stuck for a reply, and by the time he'd formed one Rebus had wandered back through the cordon, hands in trouser pockets, looking for all the world like a man out for a stroll on a balmy summer's evening. Only then did the Superintendent remember that this was Rebus's day off. He wondered if it had been such a bright idea to send him off to talk to Brigadier-General Dean. Then he smiled, recalling that he had brought John Rebus out here precisely because something didn't quite feel right. If he could feel it, Rebus would feel it too, and would burrow deep to find its source – as deep as necessary and, perhaps, deeper than was seemly for a Superintendent to go.

Yes, there were times when even Detective Inspector John Rebus came in useful.

*

It was a big house. Rebus would go further. It was bigger than the last hotel he'd stayed in, though of a similar style: closer to Hammer Films than *House and Garden*. A hotel in Scarborough it had been; three days of lust with a divorced school-dinner lady. School-dinner ladies hadn't been like that in Rebus's day . . . or maybe he just hadn't been paying attention.

He paid attention now. Paid attention as an Army uniform opened the door of West Lodge to him. He'd already had to talk his way past a mixed guard on the gate – an apologetic PC and two uncompromising squaddies. That was why he'd started thinking back to Scarborough – to stop himself punching those squaddies in their square-chinned faces. The closer he came to Brigadier-General Dean, the more aggressive and unlovely the soldiers seemed. The two on the gate were like lambs compared to the one on the main door of the house, yet he in his turn was meekness itself compared to the one who led Rebus into a well-appointed living-room and told him to wait.

Rebus hated the Army – with good reason. He had seen the soldier's lot from the inside and it had left him with a resentment so huge that to call it a 'chip on the shoulder' was to do it an injustice. Chip? Right now it felt like a whole transport café! There was only one thing for it. Rebus made for the sideboard, sniffed the contents of the decanter sitting there and poured himself an inch of whisky. He was draining the contents of the glass into his mouth when the door opened.

Rebus had brought too many preconceptions with him today. Brigadier-Generals were squat, ruddy-faced men, with stiff moustaches and VSOP noses, a few silvered wisps of Brylcreemed hair and maybe even a walking stick. They retired in their seventies and babbled of campaigns over dinner.

Not so Brigadier-General Dean. He looked to be in his mid- to late-fifties. He stood over six feet tall, had a youthful face and vigorous dark hair. He was slim too, with no sign of a retirement gut or a port drinker's red-veined cheeks.

He looked twice as fit as Rebus felt and for a moment the policeman actually caught himself straightening his back and squaring his shoulders.

'Good idea,' said Dean, joining Rebus at the sideboard. 'Mind if I join you?' His voice was soft, blurred at the edges, the voice of an educated man, a civilised man. Rebus tried hard to imagine Dean giving orders to a troop of hairy-fisted Tommies. Tried, but failed.

'Detective Inspector Rebus,' he said by way of introduction. 'Sorry to bother you like this, sir, but there are a few questions –'

Dean nodded, finishing his own drink and offering to replenish Rebus's.

'Why not?' agreed Rebus. Funny thing though: he could swear this whisky wasn't whisky at all but whiskey – Irish whiskey. Softer than the Scottish stuff, lacking an edge.

Rebus sat on the sofa, Dean on a well-used armchair. The Brigadier-General offered a toast of *slainte* before starting on his second drink, then exhaled noisily.

'Had to happen sooner or later, I suppose,' he said.

'Oh?'

Dean nodded slowly. 'I worked in Ulster for a time. Quite a long time. I suppose I was fairly high up in the tree there. I always knew I was a target. The Army knew, too, of course, but what can you do? You can't put bodyguards on every soldier who's been involved in the conflict, can you?'

'I suppose not, sir. But I assume you took precautions?'

Dean shrugged. 'I'm not in *Who's Who* and I've got an unlisted telephone number. I don't even use my rank much, to be honest.'

'But some of your mail might be addressed to Brigadier-General Dean?'

A wry smile. 'Who gave you that impression?'

'What impression, sir?'

'The impression of rank. I'm not a Brigadier-General. I retired with the rank of Major.'

'But the –'

'The what? The locals? Yes, I can see how gossip might

lead to exaggeration. You know how it is in a place like this, Inspector. An incomer who keeps himself to himself. A military air. They put two and two together then multiply it by ten.'

Rebus nodded thoughtfully. 'I see.' Trust Watson to be wrong even in the fundamentals. 'But the point I was trying to make about your mail still stands, sir. What I'm wondering, you see, is how they found you.'

Dean smiled quietly. 'The IRA are quite sophisticated these days, Inspector. For all I know, they could have hacked into a computer, bribed someone in the know, or maybe it was just a fluke, sheer chance.' He shrugged. 'I suppose we'll have to think of moving somewhere else now, starting all over again. Poor Jacqueline.'

'Jacqueline being?'

'My daughter. She's upstairs, terribly upset. She's due to start university in October. It's her I feel sorry for.'

Rebus looked sympathetic. He felt sympathetic. One thing about Army life and police life – both could have a devastating effect on your personal life.

'And your wife, sir?'

'Dead, Inspector. Several years ago.' Dean examined his now empty glass. He looked his years now, looked like someone who needed a rest. But there was something other about him, something cool and hard. Rebus had met all types in the Army – and since. Veneers could no longer fool him, and behind Major Dean's sophisticated veneer he could glimpse something other, something from the man's past. Dean hadn't just been a good soldier. At one time he'd been lethal.

'Do you have any thoughts on how they might have found you, sir?'

'Not really.' Dean closed his eyes for a second. There was resignation in his voice. 'What matters is that they *did* find me.' His eyes met Rebus's. 'And they can find me again.'

Rebus shifted in his seat. Christ, what a thought. What a, well, time-bomb. To be always watching, always expecting, always fearing. And not just for yourself.

'I'd like to talk to Jacqueline, sir. It may be that she'll have some inkling as to how they were able to –'

But Dean was shaking his head. 'Not just now, Inspector. Not yet. I don't want her – well, you understand. Besides, I'd imagine that this will all be out of your hands by tomorrow. I believe some people from the Anti-Terrorist Branch are on their way up here. Between them and the Army . . . well, as I say, it'll be out of your hands.'

Rebus felt himself prickling anew. But Dean was right, wasn't he? Why strain yourself when tomorrow it would be someone else's weight? Rebus pursed his lips, nodded, and stood up.

'I'll see you to the door,' said the Major, taking the empty glass from Rebus's hand.

As they passed into the hallway, Rebus caught a glimpse of a young woman – Jacqueline Dean presumably. She had been hovering by the telephone-table at the foot of the staircase, but was now starting up the stairs themselves, her hand thin and white on the bannister. Dean, too, watched her go. He half-smiled, half-shrugged at Rebus.

'She's upset,' he explained unnecessarily. But she hadn't looked upset to Rebus. She had looked like she was moping.

The next morning, Rebus went back to Barnton. Wooden boards had been placed over some of the shop windows, but otherwise there were few signs of yesterday's drama. The guards on the gate to West Lodge had been replaced by beefy plainclothes men with London accents. They carried portable radios, but otherwise might have been bouncers, debt collectors or bailiffs. They radioed the house. Rebus couldn't help thinking that a shout might have done the job for them, but they were in love with technology; you could see that by the way they held their radio-sets. He'd seen soldiers holding a new gun the same way.

'The guvnor's coming down to see you,' one of the men said at last. Rebus kicked his heels for a full minute before the man arrived.

'What do you want?'

'Detective Inspector Rebus. I talked with Major Dean

yesterday and –'

The man snapped. 'Who told you his rank?'

'Major Dean himself. I just wondered if I might –'

'Yes, well there's no need for that, Inspector. We're in charge now. Of course you'll be kept informed.'

The man turned and walked back through the gates with a steady, determined stride. The guards were smirking as they closed the gates behind their 'guvnor'. Rebus felt like a snubbed schoolboy, left out of the football game. Sides had been chosen and there he stood, unwanted. He could smell London on these men, that cocky superiority of a self-chosen elite. What did they call themselves? C13 or somesuch, the Anti-Terrorist Branch. Closely linked to Special Branch, and everyone knew the trade name for Special Branch – Smug Bastards.

The man had been a little younger than Rebus, well-groomed and accountant-like. More intelligent, for sure, than the gorillas on the gate, but probably well able to handle himself. A neat pistol might well have been hidden under the arm of his close-fitting suit. None of that mattered. What mattered was that the captain was leaving Rebus out of his team. It rankled; and when something rankled, it rankled hard.

Rebus had walked half a dozen paces away from the gates when he half-turned and stuck his tongue out at the guards. Then, satisfied with this conclusion to his morning's labours, he decided to make his own inquiries. It was eleven thirty. If you want to find out about someone, reasoned a thirsty Rebus, visit his local.

The reasoning, in this case, proved false: Dean had never been near the Claymore.

'The daughter came in though,' commented one young man. There weren't many people in the pub at this early stage of the day, save a few retired gentlemen who were in conversation with three or four reporters. The barman, too, was busy telling his life story to a young female hack, or rather, into her tape recorder. This made getting served difficult, despite the absence of a lunchtime scrum. The young man had solved this problem, however, reaching behind the bar to refill his glass with a mixture of cider and lager, leaving money on the bartop.

'Oh?' Rebus nodded towards the three-quarters-full glass. 'Have another?'

'When this one's finished I will.' He drank greedily, by which time the barman had finished with his confessions – much (judging by her face) to the relief of the reporter. 'Pint of Snakebite, Paul,' called the young man. When the drink was before him, he told Rebus that his name was Willie Barr and that he was unemployed.

'You said you saw the daughter in here?' Rebus was anxious to have his questions answered before the alcohol took effect on Barr.

'That's right. She came in pretty regularly.'

'By herself?'

'No, always with some guy.'

'One in particular, you mean?'

But Willie Barr laughed, shaking his head. 'A different one every time. She's getting a bit of a name for herself. And,' he raised his voice for the barman's benefit, 'she's not even eighteen, I'd say.'

'Were they local lads?'

'None I recognised. Never really spoke to them.' Rebus swirled his glass, creating a foamy head out of nothing.

'Any Irish accents among them?'

'In here?' Barr laughed. 'Not in here. Christ, no. Actually, she hasn't been in for a few weeks, now that I think of it. Maybe her father put a stop to it, eh? I mean, how would it look in the Sunday papers? Brigadier's daughter slumming it in Barnton.'

Rebus smiled. 'It's not exactly a slum though, is it?'

'True enough, but her boyfriends . . . I mean, there was more of the car mechanic than the estate agent about them. Know what I mean?' He winked. 'Not that a bit of rough ever hurt *her* kind, eh?' Then he laughed again and suggested a game or two of pool, a pound a game or a fiver if the detective were a betting man.

But Rebus shook his head. He thought he knew now why Willie Barr was drinking so much: he was flush. And the reason he was flush was that he'd been telling his story to the papers – for a price. *Brigadier's Daughter Slumming It.* Yes, he'd been telling tales all right, but there was little chance of them reaching their intended audience. The Powers That Be would see to that.

Barr was helping himself to another pint as Rebus made to leave the premises.

It was late in the afternoon when Rebus received his visitor, the Anti-Terrorist accountant.

'A Mr Matthews to see you,' the Desk Sergeant had informed Rebus, and 'Matthews' he remained, giving no hint of rank or proof of identity. He had come, he said, to 'have it out' with Rebus.

'What were you doing in the Claymore?'

'Having a drink.'

'You were asking questions. I've already told you, Inspector Rebus, we can't have –'

'I know, I know.' Rebus raised his hands in a show of surrender. 'But the more furtive you lot are, the more interested I become.'

Matthews stared silently at Rebus. Rebus knew that the man was weighing up his options. One, of course, was to go to Farmer Watson and have Rebus warned off. But if Matthews were as canny as he looked, he would know this might have the opposite effect from that intended. Another option was to talk to Rebus, to ask him what he wanted to know.

'What do you want to know?' Matthews said at last.

'I want to know about Dean.'

Matthews sat back in his chair. 'In strictest confidence?'

Rebus nodded. 'I've never been known as a clipe.'

'A clipe?'

'Someone who tells tales,' Rebus explained. Matthews was thoughtful.

'Very well then,' he said. 'For a start, Dean is an alias, a very necessary one. During his time in the Army Major Dean worked in Intelligence, mostly in West Germany but also for a time in Ulster. His work in both spheres was very important, crucially important. I don't need to go into details. His last posting was West Germany. His wife was killed in a terrorist attack, almost certainly IRA. We don't think they had targeted her specifically. She was just in the wrong place with the wrong number plates.'

'A car bomb?'

'No, a bullet. Through the windscreen, point-blank. Major Dean asked to be . . . he was invalided out. It seemed best. We provided him with a change of identity, of course.'

'I thought he looked a bit young to be retired. And the daughter, how did she take it?'

'She was never told the full details, not that I'm aware of. She was in boarding school in England.' Matthews paused. 'It was for the best.'

Rebus nodded. 'Of course, nobody'd argue with that. But why did – Dean – choose to live in Barnton?'

Matthews rubbed his left eyebrow, then pushed his spectacles back up his sharply sloping nose. 'Something to do with an aunt of his,' he said. 'He spent holidays there as a boy. His father was Army, too, posted here, there and everywhere. Never the most stable upbringing. I think Dean had happy memories of Barnton.'

Rebus shifted in his seat. He couldn't know how long Matthews would stay, how long he would continue to answer Rebus's questions. And there were so many questions.

'What about the bomb?'

'Looks like the IRA, all right. Standard fare for them, all the hallmarks. It's still being examined, of course, but we're pretty sure.'

'And the deceased?'

'No clues yet. I suppose he'll be reported missing sooner or later. We'll leave that side of things to you.'

'Gosh, thanks.' Rebus waited for his sarcasm to penetrate, then, quickly: 'How does Dean get on with his daughter?'

Matthews was caught off-guard by the question. He blinked

twice, three times, then glanced at his wristwatch.

'All right, I suppose,' he said at last, making show of scratching a mark from his cuff. 'I can't see what . . . Look, Inspector, as I say, we'll keep you fully informed. But meantime –'

'Keep out of your hair?'

'If you want to put it like that.' Matthews stood up. 'Now I really must be getting back –'

'To London?'

Matthews smiled at the eagerness in Rebus's voice. 'To Barnton. Don't worry, Inspector, the more *you* keep out of *my* hair, the quicker I can get out of yours. Fair enough?' He shot a hand out towards Rebus, who returned the almost painful grip.

'Fair enough,' said Rebus. He ushered Matthews from the room and closed the door again, then returned to his seat. He slouched as best he could in the hard, uncomfortable chair and put his feet up on the desk, examining his scuffed shoes. He tried to feel like Sam Spade, but failed. His legs soon began to ache and he slid them from the surface of the desk. The coincidences in Dashiell Hammett had nothing on the coincidence of someone nicking a car seconds before it exploded. Someone must have been watching, ready to detonate the device. But if they were watching, how come they didn't spot that Dean, the intended victim, wasn't the one to drive off?

Either there was more to this than met the eye, or else there was less. Rebus was wary – very wary. He'd already made far too many prejudgments, had already been proved wrong too many times. Keep an open mind, that was the secret. An open mind and an inquiring one. He nodded his head slowly, his eyes on the door.

'Fair enough,' he said quietly. 'I'll keep out of your hair, Mr Matthews, but that doesn't necessarily mean I'm leaving the barber's.'

The Claymore might not have been Barnton's most salubrious establishment, but it was as Princes Street's Caledonian

Hotel in comparison with the places Rebus visited that evening. He began with the merely seedy bars, the ones where each quiet voice seemed to contain a lifetime's resentment, and then moved downwards, one rung of the ladder at a time. It was slow work; the bars tended to be in a ring around Edinburgh, sometimes on the outskirts or in the distant housing schemes, sometimes nearer the centre than most of the population would dare to think.

Rebus hadn't made many friends in his adult life, but he had his network of contacts and he was as proud of it as any grandparent would be of their extended family. They were like cousins, these contacts; mostly they knew each other, at least by reputation, but Rebus never spoke to one about another, so that the extent of the chain could only be guessed at. There were those of his colleagues who, in Major Dean's words, added two and two, then multiplied by ten. John Rebus, it was reckoned, had as big a net of 'snitches' as any copper on the force bar none.

It took four hours and an outlay of over forty pounds before Rebus started to catch a glimpse of a result. His basic question, though couched in vague and imprecise terms, was simple: have any car thieves vanished off the face of the earth since yesterday?

One name was uttered by three very different people in three distinct parts of the city: Brian Cant. The name meant little to Rebus.

'It wouldn't,' he was told. 'Brian only shifted across here from the west a year or so ago. He's got form from when he was a nipper, but he's grown smart since then. When the Glasgow cops started sniffing, he moved operations.' The detective listened, nodded, drank a watered-down whisky, and said little. Brian Cant grew from a name into a description, from a description into a personality. But there was something more.

'You're not the only one interested in him,' Rebus was told in a bar in Gorgie. 'Somebody else was asking questions a wee while back. Remember Jackie Hanson?'

'He used to be CID, didn't he?'

'That's right, but not any more . . .'

Not just any old banger for Brian Cant: he specialised in 'quality motors'. Rebus eventually got an address: a third-floor tenement flat near Powderhall race-track. A young man answered the door. His name was Jim Cant, Brian's younger brother. Rebus saw that Jim was scared, nervous. He chipped away at the brother quickly, explaining that he was there because he thought Brian might be dead. That he knew all about Cant's business, but that he wasn't interested in pursuing this side of things, except insofar as it might shed light on the death. It took a little more of this, then the brother opened up.

'He said he had a customer interested in a car,' Jim Cant explained. 'An Irishman, he said.'

'How did he know the man was Irish?'

'Must have been the voice. I don't think they met. Maybe they did. The man was interested in a specific car.'

'A red Jaguar?'

'Yeah, convertible. Nice cars. The Irishman even knew where there was one. It seemed a cinch, that's what Brian kept saying. A cinch.'

'He didn't think it would be hard to steal?'

'Five seconds' work, that's what he kept saying. I thought it sounded too easy. I told him so.' He bent over in his chair, grabbing at his knees and sinking his head between them. 'Ach, Brian, what the hell have you done?'

Rebus tried to comfort the young man as best he could with brandy and tea. He drank a mug of tea himself, wandering through the flat, his mind thrumming. Was he blowing things up out of all proportion? Maybe. He'd made mistakes before, not so much errors of judgment as errors of jumping the gun. But there was something about all of this . . . Something.

'Do you have a photo of Brian?' he asked as he was leaving. 'A recent one would be best.' Jim Cant handed him a holiday snap.

'We went to Crete last summer,' he explained. 'It was magic.' Then, holding the door open for Rebus: 'Don't I have to identify him or something?'

Rebus thought of the scrapings which were all that remained of what may or may not have been Brian Cant. He shook his head. 'I'll let you know,' he said. 'If we need you, we'll let you know.'

The next day was Sunday, day of rest. Rebus rested in his car, parked fifty yards or so along the road from the gates to West Lodge. He put his radio on, folded his arms and sank down into the driver's seat. This was more like it. The Hollywood private eye on a stakeout. Only in the movies, a stakeout could be whittled away to a few minutes' footage. Here, it was measured in a slow ticking of seconds . . . minutes . . . quarter hours.

Eventually, the gates opened and a figure hurried out, fairly trotting along the pavement as though released from bondage. Jacqueline Dean was wearing a denim jacket, short black skirt and thick black tights. A beret sat awkwardly on her cropped dark hair and she pressed the palm of her hand to it from time to time to stop it sliding off altogether. Rebus locked his car before following her. He kept to the other side of the road, wary not so much from fear that she might spot him but because C13 might have put a tail on her, too.

She stopped at the local newsagent's first and came out heavy-laden with Sunday papers. Rebus, making to cross the road, a Sunday-morning stroller, studied her face. What was the expression he'd thought of the first time he'd seen her? Yes, *moping*. There was still something of that in her liquid eyes, the dark shadows beneath. She was making for the corner shop now. Doubtless she would appear with rolls or bacon or butter or milk. All the things Rebus seemed to find himself short of on a Sunday, no matter how hard he planned.

He felt in his jacket pockets, but found nothing of comfort there, just the photograph of Brian Cant. The window of the corner shop, untouched by the blast, contained a dozen or so personal ads, felt-tipped onto plain white postcards. He glanced at these, and past them, through the window itself to where Jacqueline was making her purchases. Milk and rolls: elementary, my dear Conan Doyle. Waiting for her change, she half-turned her head towards the window. Rebus concentrated on the postcards. 'Candy, Masseuse' vied for attention with 'Pram and carry-cot for sale', 'Babysitting considered', and 'Lada, seldom used'. Rebus was smiling, almost despite himself, when the door of the shop tinkled open.

'Jacqueline?' he said. She turned towards him. He was holding open his ID. 'Mind if I have a word, Miss Dean?'

Major Dean was pouring himself a glass of Irish whiskey when the drawing-room door opened.

'Mind if I come in?' Rebus's words were directed not at Dean but at Matthews, who was seated in a chair by the window, one leg crossed over the other, hands gripping the arm-rests. He looked like a nervous businessman on an airplane, trying not to let his neighbour see his fear.

'Inspector Rebus,' he said tonelessly. 'I thought I could feel my scalp tingle.'

Rebus was already in the room. He closed the door behind him. Dean gestured with the decanter, but Rebus shook his head.

'How did you get in?' Matthews asked.

'Miss Dean was good enough to escort me through the gate. You've changed the guard detail again. She told them I was a friend of the family.'

Matthews nodded. 'And are you, Inspector? Are you a friend of the family?'

'That depends on what you mean by friendship.'

Dean had seated himself on the edge of his chair, steadying the glass with both hands. He didn't seem quite the figure he had been on the day of the explosion. A reaction, Rebus didn't doubt. There had been a quiet euphoria on the day; now came the aftershock.

'Where's Jacqui?' Dean asked, having paused with the glass to his lips.

'Upstairs,' Rebus explained. 'I thought it would be better

if she didn't hear this.'

Matthews' fingers plucked at the arm-rests. 'How much does she know?'

'Not much. Not yet. Maybe she'll work it out for herself.'

'So, Inspector, we come to the reason why you're here.'

'I'm here,' Rebus began, 'as part of a murder inquiry. I thought that's why you were here, too, Mr Matthews. Maybe I'm wrong. Maybe you're here to cover up rather than bring to light.'

Matthews' smile was momentary. But he said nothing.

'I didn't go looking for the culprits,' Rebus went on. 'As you said, Mr Matthews, that was *your* department. But I did wonder who the victim was. The accidental victim, as I thought. A young car thief called Brian Cant, that would be my guess. He stole cars to order. A client asked him for a red open-top Jag, even told him where he might find one. The client told him about Major Dean. Very specifically about Major Dean, right down to the fact that every day he'd nip into the wine-shop on the main street.' Rebus turned to Dean. 'A bottle of Irish a day, is it, sir?'

Dean merely shrugged and drained his glass.

'Anyway, that's what your daughter told me. So all Brian Cant had to do was wait near the wine-shop. You'd get out of your car, leave it running, and while you were in the shop he could drive the car away. Only it bothered me that the client – Cant's brother tells me he spoke with an Irish accent – knew so much, making it easy for Cant. What was stopping this person from stealing the car himself?'

'And the answer came to you?' Matthews suggested, his voice thick with irony.

Rebus chose to avoid his tone. He was still watching Dean. 'Not straight away, not even then. But when I came to the house, I couldn't help noticing that Miss Dean seemed a bit strange. Like she was waiting for a phone call from someone and that someone had let her down. It's easy to be specific now, but at the time it just struck me as odd. I asked her about it this morning and she admitted it's because she's been jilted. A man she'd been seeing, and seeing regularly, had suddenly stopped calling. I asked her about him, but she couldn't be very helpful. They never went to his flat, for example. He drove a flashy car and had plenty of money, but she was vague about what he did for a living.'

Rebus took a photograph from his pocket and tossed it into Dean's lap. Dean froze, as though it were some hair-trigger grenade.

'I showed her a photograph of Brian Cant. Yes, that was the name of her boyfriend – Brian Cant. So you see, it was small wonder she hadn't heard from him.'

Matthews rose from the chair and stood before the window itself, but nothing he saw there seemed to please him, so he turned back into the room. Dean had found the courage to lift the photograph from his leg and place it on the floor. He got up too, and made for the decanter.

'For Christ's sake,' Matthews hissed, but Dean poured regardless.

Rebus's voice was level. 'I always thought it was a bit of a coincidence, the car being stolen only seconds before exploding. But then the IRA use remote control devices, don't they? So that someone in the vicinity could have triggered the bomb any time they liked. No need for all these long-term timers and what have you. I was in the SAS once myself.'

Matthews raised an eyebrow. 'Nobody told me that,' he said, sounding impressed for the first time.

'So much for Intelligence, eh?' Rebus answered. 'Speaking of which, you told me that Major Dean here was in Intelligence. I think I'd go further. Covert operations, that sort of thing? Counter-intelligence, subversion?'

'Now you're speculating, Inspector.'

Rebus shrugged. 'It doesn't really matter. What matters is that someone had been spying on Brian Cant, an ex-policeman called Jackie Hanson. He's a private detective these days. He won't say anything about his clients, of course, but I think I can put two and two together without multiplying the result. He was working for you, Major Dean, because you were interested in Brian Cant. Jacqueline was serious about him, wasn't she? So much so that she might have forsaken university. She tells me they were even talking of moving in together. You didn't want her to leave. When you found out what Cant did for a . . . a living, I suppose you'd call it, you came up with a plan.' Rebus was enjoying himself now, but tried to keep the pleasure out of his voice.

'You contacted Cant,' he went on, 'putting on an Irish accent. Your Irish accent is probably pretty good, isn't it, Major? It would need to be, working in counterintelligence. You told him all about a car – your car. You offered him a lot of money if he'd steal it for you and you told him precisely when and where he might find it. Cant was greedy. He didn't think twice.' Rebus noticed that he was sitting very comfortably in his own chair, whereas Dean looked. . . the word that sprang to mind was 'rogue'. Matthews, too, was sparking internally, though his surface was all metal sheen, cold bodywork.

'You'd know how to make a bomb, that goes without saying. Wouldn't you, Major? Know thine enemy and all that. Like I say, I was in the SAS myself. What's more, you'd know how to make an IRA device, or one that looked like the work of the IRA. The remote was in your pocket. You went into the shop, bought your whiskey, and when you heard the car being driven off, you simply pressed the button.'

'Jacqueline.' Dean's voice was little more than a whisper. 'Jacqueline.' He rose to his feet, walked softly to the door and left the room. He appeared to have heard little or nothing of Rebus's speech. Rebus felt a pang of disappointment and looked towards Matthews, who merely shrugged.

'You cannot, of course, prove any of this, Inspector.'

'If I put my mind to it I can.'

'Oh, I've no doubt, no doubt.' Matthews paused. 'But will you?'

'He's mad, you've got to see that.'

'Mad? Well, he's unstable. Ever since his wife . . . '

'No reason for him to murder Brian Cant.' Rebus helped himself to a whisky now, his legs curiously shaky. 'How long have you known?'

Matthews shrugged again. 'He tried a similar trick in

Germany, apparently. It didn't work that time. So what do we do now? Arrest him? He'd be unfit to plead.'

'However it happens,' Rebus said, 'he's got to be made safe.'

'Absolutely.' Matthews was nodding agreement. He came to the sideboard. 'A hospital, somewhere he can be treated. He was a good soldier in his day. I've read his record. A good soldier. Don't worry, Inspector Rebus, he'll be 'made safe' as you put it. He'll be taken care of.' A hand landed on Rebus's forearm. 'Trust me.'

Rebus trusted Matthews – about as far as he could spit into a Lothian Road headwind. He had a word with a reporter friend, but the man wouldn't touch the story. He passed Rebus on to an investigative journalist who did some ferreting, but there was little or nothing to be found. Rebus didn't know Dean's real name. He didn't know Matthews' first name or rank or even, to be honest, that he had been C13 at all. He might have been Army, or have inhabited that indefinite smear of operations somewhere between Army, Secret Service and Special Branch.

By the next day, Dean and his daughter had left West Lodge and a fortnight later it appeared in the window of an estate agent on George Street. The asking price seemed surprisingly low, if your tastes veered towards *The Munsters*. But the house would stay in the window for a long time to come.

Dean haunted Rebus's dreams for a few nights, no more. But how did you make safe a man like that? The Army had designed a weapon and that weapon had become maladjusted, its sights all wrong. You could dismantle a weapon. You could dismantle a man, too, come to that. But each and every piece was still as lethal as the whole. Rebus put aside fiction, put aside Hammett and the rest and of an evening read psychology books instead. But then they too, in their way, were fiction, weren't they? And so, too, in time became the case that was not a case of the man who had never been.

The Naming of the Dead
Introduction and Chapter 1

G8 . . . George Bush . . . Rebus . . .

The Naming of the Dead is a potent mix of action and politics, set against a backdrop of the most devastating week in recent British history.

Set in July 2005 when the G8 leaders gathered in Scotland. Facing daily marches, demonstrations, and scuffles, the police are at full stretch. Detective Inspector John Rebus, however, has been sidelined, until the apparent suicide of an MP coincides with clues that a serial killer may be on the loose. The authorities are keen to hush up both, for fear of overshadowing a meeting of global importance – but Rebus has never been one to stick to the rules, and when his colleague Siobhan Clarke finds herself hunting down the identity of the riot cop who assaulted her mother, it looks as though Rebus and Clarke may be pitted against both sides in the conflict.

'Masterly . . . Ian Rankin's finest novel. It is more than a crime novel, or rather, Rankin's achievement is to show, convincingly, how crime permeates society'
Scotsman

'His richest and most complex work to date, it comes close to transcending genre fiction'
Scotland on Sunday

Coming in paperback July 2007

Ian on *The Naming of the Dead*

I got the idea for *The Naming of the Dead* in June 2005. I had started reading lots of media scare stories about the forthcoming G8 meeting of world leaders in Scotland, and thought the whole G8 week might make an intriguing backdrop to a novel. It also amused me that amidst rumours of police reinforcements, limitless overtime for cops, etc, Rebus would be the one detective left out of proceedings – there was no way his bosses would want such a troublemaker anywhere near the G8. I stayed in Edinburgh during the whole of G8 week, taking notes, and then headed off on holiday to an area of Scotland north of Inverness called the Black Isle. Had a whale of a time, and also came across a creepy spot called the Clootie Well. It's a glade with a small spring emerging from the ground, and local people down the years have left pieces of clothing there for luck – the trees were draped with decaying t-shirts and pants and socks; all very strange. I thought: what a great place for a body! But Black Isle was too remote to make it accessible to Rebus, so I decided to 'move' the Clootie Well to Auchterarder, home of Gleneagles (which just happened to be where the G8 leaders had met). Suddenly, Rebus had a reason for visiting the G8 . . . the story was up and running. Then I looked back over my notes, and remembered that some marchers had climbed to the top of Edinburgh's Calton Hill to commemorate the lives lost during the Iraq conflict, in a ceremony they called 'Naming the Dead'. Thanks to them, I now had my title, too, though the book itself would take a further nine months to write. But I'm pleased with the results – dead pleased.

Ian Rankin

THE NAMING OF THE DEAD

chapter 1

In place of a closing hymn, there was music. The Who, 'Love Reign O'er Me'. Rebus recognised it the moment it started, thunderclaps and teeming rain filling the chapel. He was in the front pew; Chrissie had insisted. He'd rather have been further back: his usual place at funerals. Chrissie's son and daughter sat next to her. Lesley was comforting her mother, an arm around her as the tears fell. Kenny stared straight ahead, storing up emotion for later. Earlier that morning, back at the house, Rebus had asked him his age. He would be thirty next month. Lesley was two years younger. Brother and sister looked like their mother, reminding Rebus that people had said the same about Michael and him: *The pair of you, the spit of your mum.* Michael . . . Mickey if you preferred. Rebus's younger brother, dead in a shiny-handled box at the age of fifty-four, Scotland's mortality rate that of a Third World nation. Lifestyle, diet, genes – plenty of theories. The full post-mortem hadn't come through yet. Massive stroke was what Chrissie had told Rebus on the phone, assuring him that it was 'sudden' – as if that made a difference.

Sudden meant Rebus hadn't been able to say goodbye. It meant his last words to Michael had been a joke about his beloved Raith Rovers in a phone call three months back. A Raith scarf, navy and white, had been draped over the coffin alongside the wreaths. Kenny was wearing a tie that had been his dad's, Raith's shield on it – some kind of animal holding a belt-buckle. Rebus had asked the significance, but Kenny had just shrugged. Looking along the pew, Rebus saw the usher make a gesture. Everyone rose to their feet. Chrissie started walking up the aisle, flanked by her children. The usher looked to Rebus, but he stayed where he was. Sat down again so the others would know they didn't have to wait for him. The song was only a little over halfway through. It was the closing track on *Quadrophenia*. Michael had been the big Who fan, Rebus himself preferring the Stones. Had to admit, though, albums like *Tommy* and *Quadrophenia* did things the Stones never could. Daltrey was whooping that he could use a drink. Rebus had to agree, but there was the drive back to Edinburgh to consider.

The function room of a local hotel had been booked. All were welcome, as the minister had reminded them from the pulpit. Whisky and tea would be poured, sandwiches served. There would be anecdotes and reminiscences, smiles, dabs at the eyes, hushed tones. The staff would move quietly, out of respect. Rebus was trying to form sentences in his head, words which would act as his apology.

I need to get back, Chrissie. Pressure of work.

He could lie and blame the G8. That morning in the house, Lesley had said he must be busy with the build-up. He could have told her, *I'm the only cop they don't seem to need.* Officers were being drafted in from all over. Fifteen hundred were coming from London alone. Yet Detective Inspector John Rebus seemed surplus to requirements. Someone had to man the ship – the very words DCI James Macrae had used, with his acolyte smirking by his shoulder. DI Derek Starr reckoned himself the heir apparent to Macrae's throne. One day he'd be running Gayfield Square police station. John Rebus posed no threat whatsoever, not much more than a year away from retirement. Starr himself had said as much: *Nobody'd blame you for coasting, John. It's what anyone your age would do.* Maybe so, but the Stones were older than Rebus; Daltrey and Townshend were older than him too. Still playing, still touring.

The song was ending now, and Rebus rose to his feet again. He was alone in the chapel. Took a final look at the purple velvet screen. Maybe the coffin was still behind it; maybe it had already been moved to another part of the crematorium. He thought back to adolescence, two brothers in their shared bedroom, playing 45s bought down Kirkcaldy High Street. 'My Generation' and 'Substitute', Mickey asking about Daltrey's stutter on the former, Rebus saying he'd read somewhere that it was to do with drugs. The only drug the brothers had indulged in was alcohol, mouthfuls stolen from the bottles in the pantry, a can of sickly stout broken open and shared after lights-out. Standing on Kirkcaldy promenade, staring out to sea, and Mickey singing the words to 'I Can See For Miles'. But could that really have happened? The record came out in '66 or '67, by which time Rebus was in the army. Must have been on a trip back. Yes, Mickey with his shoulder-length hair, trying to copy Daltrey's look, and Rebus with his forces crop, inventing stories to make army life seem exciting, Northern Ireland still ahead of him . . .

They'd been close back then, Rebus always sending letters and postcards, his father proud of him, proud of both the boys.

The spit of your mum.

He stepped outside. The cigarette packet was already open in his hand. There were other smokers around him. They offered nods, shuffling their feet. The various wreaths and cards had been lined up next to the door, and were being studied by the mourners. The usual words would crop up: 'condolence' and 'loss' and 'sorrow'. The family would be 'in our thoughts'. Michael wouldn't be mentioned by name. Death brought its own set of protocols. The younger mourners were checking for text messages on their phones. Rebus dug his own out of his pocket and switched it on. Five missed calls, all from the same number. Rebus knew it from memory, pushed the buttons and raised the phone to his ear. Detective Sergeant Siobhan Clarke was quick to answer.

'I've been trying you all morning,' she complained.

'I had it switched off.'

'Where are you anyway?'

'Still in Kirkcaldy.'

There was an intake of breath. 'Hell, John, I completely forgot.'

'Don't worry about it.' He watched Kenny open the car door for Chrissie. Lesley was motioning to Rebus, letting him know they were headed for the hotel. The car was a BMW, Kenny doing all right for himself as a mechanical engineer. He wasn't married; had a girlfriend but she hadn't been able to make it to the funeral. Lesley was divorced, her own son and daughter off on holiday with their dad. Rebus nodded at her as she got into the back of the car.

'I thought it was next week,' Siobhan was saying.

'I take it you're phoning for a gloat?' Rebus started walking towards his Saab. Siobhan had been in Perthshire the past two days, accompanying Macrae on a recce of G8 security. Macrae was old pals with Tayside's Assistant Chief Constable. All Macrae wanted was a nosy, his friend happy to oblige. The G8 leaders would meet at Gleneagles Hotel, on the outskirts of Auchterarder, nothing around them but acres of wilderness and miles of ring-fenced security. There had been plenty of scare stories in the media. Reports of three thousand US Marines landing in Scotland to protect their president. Anarchist plots to block roads and bridges with hijacked trucks. Bob Geldof had demanded that a million demonstrators besiege Edinburgh. They would be housed, he said, in people's spare rooms, garages and gardens. Boats would be sent to France to pick up protesters. Groups with names like Ya Basta and the Black Bloc would aim for chaos, while the People's Golfing Association wanted to break the cordon to play a few holes of Gleneagles' renowned course.

'I'm spending two days with DCI Macrae,' Siobhan was saying. 'What's to gloat about?'

Rebus unlocked his car, and leaned in to slide the key into the ignition. He straightened again, took a last drag on his cigarette and flicked the butt on to the roadway. Siobhan was saying something about a Scene of Crime team.

'Hold on,' Rebus told her. 'I didn't catch that.'

'Look, you've got enough on your plate without this.'

'Without what?'

'Remember Cyril Colliar?'

'Despite my advancing years, the memory's not quite

packed in.'

'Something really strange has happened.'

'What?'

'I think I've found the missing piece.'

'Of what?'

'The jacket.'

Rebus found that he'd lowered himself on to the driver's seat. 'I don't understand.'

Siobhan gave a nervous laugh. 'Me neither.'

'So where are you now?'

'Auchterarder.'

'And that's where the jacket's turned up?'

'Sort of.'

Rebus swung his legs into the car and pulled the door shut. 'Then I'm coming to take a look. Is Macrae with you?'

'He went to Glenrothes. That's where the G8 control centre is.' She paused. 'Are you sure you should be doing this?'

Rebus had started the engine. 'I need to make my apologies first, but I can be there inside the hour. Will I have any trouble getting into Auchterarder?'

'It's the calm before the storm. When you're driving through town, look for the sign to the Clootie Well.'

'The what?'

'Easier if you just come and see for yourself.'

'Then that's what I'll do. Scene of Crime on their way?'

'Yes.'

'Which means word will get around.'

'Should I tell the DCI?'

'I'll let you decide.' Rebus had wedged the phone between his shoulder and his cheek, so he could steer the mazy course to the gates of the crematorium.

'You're breaking up,' Siobhan said.

Not if I can help it, Rebus thought to himself.

Cyril Colliar had been murdered six weeks before. Aged twenty, he'd been locked away on a fixed ten-year stretch for a vicious rape. At the end of the sentence, he'd been released, despite the reservations of prison warders, police and social services. They reckoned he was as big a threat as ever, having shown no remorse, denying his guilt despite DNA evidence. Colliar had returned to his native Edinburgh. All the body-building he'd done in prison paid off. He worked as a night-time bouncer and daytime muscle. His employer on both counts was Morris Gerald Cafferty. 'Big Ger' was a villain of long standing. It had been Rebus's job to confront him about his latest employee.

'What do I care?' had been the retort.

'He's dangerous.'

'Way you're hassling him would try the patience of a saint.' Cafferty swinging from side to side on his leather swivel chair, behind his desk at MGC Lettings. Anyone was slow with the weekly rent on one of Cafferty's flats, Rebus reckoned that was where Colliar would take over. Cafferty ran mini-cabs too, and owned at least three raucous bars in the less salubrious parts of town. Plenty of work for Cyril Colliar.

Right up until the night he'd turned up dead. Skull caved in, the blow coming from behind. Pathologist reckoned he'd have died from that alone, but just to make sure, someone had added a syringe of very pure heroin. No indication that the deceased had been a user. 'Deceased' was the word most of the cops on the case had used – and grudgingly at that. Nobody bothered with the term 'victim'. Nobody could say the words out loud – *bastard got what he deserved* – that wasn't the done thing these days.

Didn't stop them thinking it, sharing it through eye contact and slow nods. Rebus and Siobhan had worked the case, but it had been one amongst many. Few leads and too many suspects. The rape victim had been interviewed, along with her family and her boyfriend from the time. One word kept coming up in discussing Colliar's fate.

'Good.'

His body had been found near his car, down a side street next to the bar he'd been working. No witnesses, no scene-of-crime evidence. Just the one curiosity: a sharp blade had been used to slice away part of his distinctive jacket. It was a black nylon bomber, emblazoned with the phrase

CC Rider on the back. This was what had been removed, so that the white inner lining was revealed. Theories were in short supply. It was either a clumsy attempt to disguise the deceased's identity, or there had been something hidden in the lining. Tests had proved negative for traces of drugs, leaving the police to shrug and scratch their heads.

To Rebus, it looked like a hit. Either Colliar had made an enemy, or a message was being sent to Cafferty. Not that their several interviews with Colliar's employer had been enlightening.

'Bad for my reputation,' was Cafferty's main reaction. 'Means either you catch whoever did it . . .'

'Or?'

But Cafferty hadn't needed to answer. And if Cafferty got to the culprit first, it would be the last that was ever heard of them.

None of which had helped. The inquiry had hit a wall, around the same time G8 preparations started focussing minds – most of them driven by images of overtime pay – elsewhere. Other cases had intruded, too, with victims – *real* victims. The Colliar murder team had been wound down.

Rebus lowered his driver's-side window, welcoming the cool breeze. He didn't know the quickest route to Auchterarder; knew Gleneagles could be reached from Kinross, so had headed that way. A couple of months back, he'd bought satnav for the car, but hadn't got round to reading the instructions yet. It lay on the passenger seat, screen blank. One of these days he'd take it to the garage which had installed the car's CD player. An inspection of the back seat, floors and boot had failed to turn up anything by The Who, so Rebus was listening to Elbow instead – Siobhan's recommendation. He liked the title track, 'Leaders of the Free World'. Stuck it on repeat. The singer seemed to think something had gone wrong since the sixties. Rebus tended to agree, even coming at it from a different direction. He reckoned the singer would have liked more change, a world run by Greenpeace and CND, poverty made history. Rebus had been on a few marches himself in the sixties, before and after joining the army. It was a way to meet girls, if nothing else. Usually there was a party somewhere afterwards. These days, though, he saw the sixties as the end of something. A fan had been stabbed to death at a Stones concert in 1969, and the decade had petered out. The 1960s had given youth a taste for revolt. They didn't trust the old order, certainly didn't respect it. He wondered about the thousands who would descend on Gleneagles, confrontation a racing certainty. Hard to imagine it in this landscape of farms and hillsides, rivers and glens. He knew that Gleneagles' very isolation would have been a factor in its choice as venue. The leaders of the free world would be safe there, safe to sign their names to decisions which had already been taken elsewhere. On the stereo, the band were singing about climbing a landslide. The image stuck with Rebus all the way to the outskirts of Auchterarder.

He didn't think he'd been there before. All the same, he seemed to know the place. Typical small Scottish town: a single, well-defined main street with narrow side roads leading off, built to a notion that people would walk to their local shops. Small, independently owned shops at that: he didn't see much that would inflame the anti-globalisation campaigners. The baker was even selling limited edition G8 pies.

The good folk of Auchterarder, Rebus seemed to recall, had been vetted, under guise of providing them with ID badges. These would be necessary so they could cross the eventual barricades. Yet as Siobhan had pointed out, there was an eerie tranquillity to the place. Only a few shoppers, and one joiner who seemed to be measuring up windows for protective boards. The cars were muddy 4x4s, which had probably spent more time on farm tracks than motorways. One woman driver was even wearing a headscarf, something Rebus hadn't seen in a while. Within a couple of minutes he was at the far end of town and heading towards the A9. He did a three-point turn and this time kept his eyes open for signposts. The one he wanted was next to a pub, pointing down a lane. He signalled, following the road past hedges and driveways, then a newer housing estate. The landscape opened before him, showing distant hills. In moments he was out of town again, flanked by neat hedgerows which would leave their mark on his car if he had to make way for a tractor or delivery van. There were some woods to his left, and another pointer told him this was home to the Clootie Well. He knew the word from clootie dumpling: a sticky steamed dessert his mother had sometimes made. He remembered the taste and texture as being similar to Christmas pudding. Dark and cloying and sugary. His stomach gave a small protest, reminding him that he hadn't eaten in hours. His stop at the hotel had been brief, a few quiet words with Chrissie. She'd hugged him, just as she had done back at the house earlier that morning. All the years he'd known her, there hadn't been many hugs. In the early days, he'd actually fancied her; awkward under the circumstances. She'd seemed to sense this. Then he'd been best man at the wedding, and, during one dance, she'd blown mischievously in his ear. Later, on the few occasions when she and Mickey had been separated, Rebus had taken his brother's side. He supposed he could have called her, said something, but he hadn't. And when Mickey had got into that spot of bother, ended up in jail, Rebus hadn't visited Chrissie and the kids. Mind you, he hadn't visited Mickey that often either, in jail or since.

There was more history: when Rebus and his own wife had separated, Chrissie had blamed him entirely. She'd always got on well with Rhona; kept in touch with her after the divorce. That was family for you. Tactics, campaigning and diplomacy: the politicians had it easy by comparison.

Back at the hotel, Lesley had mimicked her mother, giving him a hug too. Kenny had thought for a second before Rebus put the lad out of his misery by extending a hand to be squeezed. He wondered if there would be any fallings-out; there usually were at funerals. With grief came blame and resentment. Just as well he hadn't stayed. When it came to the potential for confrontation, John Rebus punched well above his already substantial weight.

There was a parking area just off the road. It looked like

new-build, trees having been cleared, chippings of bark strewn across the ground. Room enough for four cars, but only one was waiting. Siobhan Clarke was leaning against it, arms folded. Rebus pulled on the brake and got out.

'Nice spot,' he said.

'Been here over a hundred years,' she told him.

'Didn't think I drove that slowly.'

She offered only a twist of the mouth, leading him into the woods, arms still folded. She was dressed more formally than usual: knee-length black skirt and black tights. Her shoes were smudged, having walked this same trail earlier.

'I saw the sign yesterday,' she was saying. 'The one leading off the main drag. Decided I'd take a look.'

'Well, if the choice was that or Glenrothes . . .'

'There's a noticeboard back at the clearing, tells you a bit about the place. All sorts of witchy goings-on down the years.' They were ascending a slope, rounding a thick, twisted oak. 'The townspeople decided there must be sprites living here: shrieks in the dark, that sort of thing.'

'Local farmhands more like,' Rebus offered.

She nodded agreement. 'All the same, they started leaving little offerings. Hence the name.' She glanced around at him. 'You'll know what clootie means, you being the only native Scot around here?'

He had a sudden image of his mother lifting the pudding out of its pan. The pudding wrapped in . . .

'Cloth,' he told her.

'And clothing,' she added as they entered another clearing. They stopped and Rebus breathed deeply. Damp cloth . . . damp, rotting cloth. He'd been smelling it for the past half-minute. The smell clothes gave off in his old house, the one he'd grown up in, when they weren't aired, when the damp and the mildew got to them. The trees around him were strung with rags and remnants. Pieces had fallen to the ground, where they were decomposing to a mulch.

'Tradition has it,' Siobhan said quietly, 'they were left here for good luck. Keep the sprites warm, and they'd see no harm came to you. Another theory: when kids died young, their parents left something here, by way of remembrance.' Her voice caught, and she cleared her throat.

'I'm not made of glass,' Rebus assured her. 'You can use words like "remembrance" – I'm not going to start blubbing.'

She nodded again. Rebus was walking around the clearing. Leaves and soft moss underfoot, and the sound of a stream, just a thin trickle of water pushing up from the ground. Candles and coins had been left by its edges.

'Not much of a well,' he commented.

She just shrugged. 'I was here a few minutes. . . didn't really warm to the atmosphere. But then I noticed some of the newer clothing.' Rebus saw it too. Strung from the branches. A shawl, a boilersuit, a red polka-dot handkerchief. A nearly-new training shoe, its laces dangling. Even underwear and what looked like children's tights.

'Christ, Siobhan,' Rebus muttered, not really knowing what else to say. The smell seemed to be growing stronger. He had another flashback: to a ten-day bender many years before . . . coming out of it to find that a load of washing had been sitting in the machine, waiting to be hung. When he'd opened the door, this same smell had hit him. He'd washed everything again, but still had to throw it all away afterwards. 'And the jacket?'

All she did was point. Rebus walked slowly towards the tree in question. The piece of nylon had been pierced by a short branch. It swayed just a little in the breeze. Threads straggling from it, but no mistaking the logo.

'*CC Rider*,' Rebus said in confirmation. Siobhan was running her hands through her hair. He knew she had questions, knew she would have been turning them over in her mind all the time she'd been waiting for him. 'So what do we do?' he prompted.

'It's a crime scene,' she began. 'A team are on their way from Stirling. We need to secure the locus, comb the area for evidence. We need to reassemble the original murder squad, start doorstepping locally . . .'

'Including Gleneagles?' Rebus interrupted. 'You're the expert, so you tell me: how many times have the hotel staff been vetted? And how do we go about doorstepping in the middle of a week-long demo? Securing the locus won't be a problem, mind you, not with all the secret service teams we're about to welcome . . .'

Naturally she had considered all these points. He knew as much and his voice trailed off.

'We keep it quiet till the summit's over,' she suggested.

'Tempting,' he admitted.

She smiled. 'Only because it gives you a head start.'

He admitted as much with a wink.

She sighed. 'Macrae needs to be told. Which means he'll tell Tayside Police.'

'But the SOCOs are coming from Stirling,' Rebus added, 'and Stirling belongs to Central Region.'

'So that's just the three police forces who need to know . . . Shouldn't have any trouble keeping it under wraps.'

Rebus was looking around. 'If we can at least get the scene checked and photographed . . . take the cloth back to the lab . . .'

'Before the fun and games start?'

Rebus puffed out his cheeks. 'Kicks off on Wednesday, right?'

'The G8 does, yes. But there's the Poverty March tomorrow and another planned for Monday.'

'In Edinburgh, though, not Auchterarder . . .' Then he saw what she was getting at. Even with the evidence at the lab, the whole place could be under siege. Getting from Gayfield Square to the lab at Howdenhall meant crossing the city . . . always supposing the technicians had managed to force their way into work.

'Why leave it here?' Siobhan asked, studying the patch again. 'Some sort of trophy?'

'If so, why here specifically?'

'Could be local. Any family connections with the area?'

'I think Colliar's solid Edinburgh.'

She looked at him. 'I meant the rape victim.'

Rebus formed his mouth into an O.

'Something to consider,' she added. Then she paused. 'What's that sound?'

Rebus patted his stomach. 'While since I've eaten. Don't suppose Gleneagles is open for afternoon tea?'

'Depends on your overdraft. There are places in town. One of us should stay for the SOCOs.'

'Better be you then; don't want accusations that I'm hogging the limelight. In fact, you probably deserve a complimentary beaker of Auchterarder's finest tea.' He turned to go, but she stopped him.

'Why me? Why now?' Her arms stretching from her sides.

'Why not?' he answered. 'Just call it kismet.'

'That's not what I mean . . .'

He turned towards her again.

'What I mean,' she said quietly, 'is that I'm not sure I want them caught. If they are, and it's been down to me . . .'

'If they are, Shiv, it'll be down to their cock-up.' He stabbed a finger in the direction of the patch. 'That, and maybe even a bit of teamwork . . .'

The Scene of Crime unit hadn't been thrilled by the news that Rebus and Siobhan had entered the locus. Prints of their shoes had been taken, for purposes of elimination, along with hair samples.

'Go easy,' Rebus had warned. 'I can't afford to be generous.'

The SOCO had apologised. 'Got to get the root, else we can't get the DNA.' On the third try with the tweezers, he'd been successful. One of his colleagues had almost finished videoing the scene. Another was still taking photographs, and yet another was in conversation with Siobhan about how much of the other clothing they should remove to the lab.

'Just the most recent,' she told him, her eyes on Rebus. He nodded his agreement, sharing her train of thought. Even if Colliar was a message to Cafferty, didn't mean there weren't other messages here.

'Sports shirt seems to have a company logo on it,' the SOCO commented.

'Your job could hardly be easier,' Siobhan said with a smile.

'My job's collection. The rest is down to you.'

'Speaking of which,' Rebus interrupted, 'any chance this could all go to Edinburgh rather than Stirling?'

The SOCO stiffened his shoulders. Rebus didn't know him but he knew the type: late-forties, half a lifetime's experience. There was plenty of rivalry between the various police regions as it was. Rebus held up his hands in mock surrender.

'All I mean is, it's an Edinburgh case. Makes sense if they don't have to keep traipsing through to Stirling every time there's something you need to show them.'

Siobhan was smiling again, amused by his use of 'they' and 'them'. But she gave a slight nod too, recognising a useful ploy when she saw one.

'Especially now,' Rebus was arguing, 'with the demos and everything.' He looked up to where a helicopter was circling. Gleneagles surveillance, had to be. Someone up there wondering at the sudden appearance of two cars and two unmarked white vans at the Clootie Well. Returning his gaze to the SOCO, Rebus realised the chopper had sealed the deal. A time like this, co-operation was paramount. It had been hammered home in memorandum after memorandum. Macrae himself had said as much at the past dozen or so briefings at Gayfield Square.

Be nice. Work together. Help each other. Because, for these few short days, the world would be watching.

Maybe the SOCO had been at similar briefings. He was nodding slowly, turning away to continue his work. Rebus and Siobhan shared another look. Then Rebus reached into his pocket for his cigarettes.

'No traces, please,' one of the other SOCOs warned him, so Rebus moved away, back towards the car park. He was just lighting up when another car appeared. The more the merrier, he thought to himself as DCI Macrae leapt out. He was dressed in what looked like a new suit. New tie, too, and a crisp white shirt. His hair was grey and sparse, face saggy, nose bulbous and red-veined.

He's the same age as me, Rebus thought. Why does he seem so much older?

'Afternoon, sir,' Rebus said.

'Thought you were supposed to be at a funeral.' The tone was accusatory, as though Rebus might have fabricated a death in the family to secure a Friday lie-in.

'DS Clarke interrupted proceedings,' Rebus explained. 'Thought I'd show willing.' Making it sound like a sacrifice. The words worked, too, Macrae's tightened jaw relaxing a little.

I'm on a roll, Rebus thought. First the SOCO, now the boss. Macrae had been pretty good actually, green-lighting a day off for Rebus as soon as news broke of Mickey's death. He'd told Rebus to go get slaughtered, and Rebus had obliged – the Scotsman's way of dealing with death. He'd found himself in a part of town he didn't know, no idea how he got there . . . walked into a chemist's and asked where he was. Answer: Colinton Village Pharmacy. He'd thanked them by making the purchase of some aspirin . . .

'Sorry, John.' Macrae said now, taking a deep breath. 'How did it go?' Trying to sound concerned.

'It went,' was all Rebus said. He watched the helicopter bank steeply as it turned for home.

'Hope to Christ that wasn't TV,' Macrae commented.

'Not much to see, even supposing it was. Shame to tear you away from Glenrothes, sir. How's Sorbus looking?'

Operation Sorbus: the policing plan for G8 week. To Rebus, it had sounded like something a slimmer would use in their tea instead of sugar. Siobhan had put him right, told him it was a kind of tree.

'We're prepared for any eventuality,' Macrae stated briskly.

'Except maybe one,' Rebus felt it his duty to add.

'Back-burner till next week, John,' his boss muttered.

Rebus nodded his agreement. 'Always assuming *they* agree.'

Macrae followed Rebus's eye-line and saw the car approaching. It was a silver Merc with tinted rear windows.

'Probably means the chopper wasn't TV,' Rebus added for Macrae's benefit. He reached into his own car's passenger seat and brought out what remained of a filled roll. Ham salad: the first had slipped down without touching the sides.

'The hell's this?' Macrae was asking through gritted teeth. The Merc had pulled to an abrupt stop beside one of the Scene of Crime vans. The driver's door opened and a man got out. He walked around the car and tugged open the rear passenger-side door. It took several moments for the man inside to emerge. He was tall and narrow, eyes hidden behind sunglasses. As he secured all three buttons of his suit jacket, he seemed to be studying the two white vans, the three unmarked police cars. Eventually he peered up at the sky, mouthed something to his driver, and stepped away from the vehicle. Instead of approaching Rebus and Macrae, he walked over to the signpost, the one informing tourists of the Clootie Well's history. The driver was back behind his steering wheel, eyes on Rebus and Macrae. Rebus blew him a little kiss, content to stand there until the new arrival consented to make introductions. Again, he thought he knew the type: cold and calculating, making show of being the real power. Had to be security of some kind, following up the chopper's call.

Macrae took only seconds to crack. Strode over to the man and asked him who he was.

'I'm SO12, who the hell are you?' the man replied in a measured voice. Maybe he'd missed the briefings on friendly co-operation. English accent, Rebus noted. Stood to reason. SO12 was Special Branch, based in London. One step away from the spooks.

'I mean,' the man went on, his interest still apparently concentrated on the signpost, 'I know *what* you are. You're CID. And those are Scene of Crime vans. And in a clearing just ahead of us there are men in white protective overalls making a detailed examination of the trees and ground.' Finally he turned towards Macrae, and reached a slow hand to his own face to remove the sunglasses. 'How am I doing so far?'

Macrae's face had reddened in anger. All day he'd been treated with the dignity which was his due. Now this.

'Care to show some ID?' Macrae snapped. The man stared at him, then gave a wry smile. *Is that all you've got?*

the smile seemed to say. As he reached into his jacket, not bothering to unbutton it, his eyes shifted from Macrae to Rebus. The smile stayed, inviting Rebus to share its message. A small black leather wallet was held open for Macrae's inspection.

'There,' the man said, snapping it shut again. 'Now you know all there is to know about me.'

'You're Steelforth,' Macrae said, clearing his throat between words. Rebus could see his boss had been thrown. Macrae turned towards him. 'Commander Steelforth is in charge of G8 security,' he explained. But Rebus had already guessed as much. Macrae turned back to Steelforth. 'I was in Glenrothes this morning, being given a tour courtesy of ACC Finnigan. And Gleneagles yesterday . . .' Macrae's voice faltered. Steelforth was already moving away from him, towards Rebus.

'Not interrupting your coronary, am I?' he asked, glancing at the roll. Rebus gave the belch he felt the query demanded. Steelforth's eyes narrowed.

'We can't all be dining courtesy of the taxpayer,' Rebus said. 'How is the food at Gleneagles, by the way?'

'I doubt you'll get the chance to find out, Detective Sergeant.'

'Not a bad guess, sir, but your eyes deceive you.'

'This is DI Rebus,' Macrae was explaining. 'I'm DCI Macrae, Lothian and Borders.'

'Based where?' Steelforth asked.

'Gayfield Square,' Macrae answered.

'In Edinburgh,' Rebus added.

'You're a long way from home, gentlemen.' Steelforth was heading down the path.

'A man was murdered in Edinburgh,' Rebus explained. 'Some of his clothing has turned up here.'

'Do we know why?'

'I intend keeping a lid on it, Commander,' Macrae stated. 'Once the SOCOs are finished, that's us done and dusted.'

Macrae was at Steelforth's heels, Rebus bringing up the rear.

'No plans for any premiers or presidents to come leave a

wee offering?' Rebus asked.

Instead of answering, Steelforth marched into the clearing. The senior SOCO stuck a hand against the Commander's chest. 'More fucking footprints,' he growled.

Steelforth glared at the hand. 'Do you know who I am?'

'Don't give a bollocks, pal. Fuck up my crime scene, you'll answer for it.'

The Special Branch man considered for a moment, then relented, retracing his steps to the edge of the clearing, content to watch the operation. His mobile sounded, and he answered it, moving further away to prevent being overheard. Siobhan gave a questioning look. Rebus mouthed, 'Later,' and dug into his pocket, bringing out a ten-pound note.

'Here,' he said, offering it to the SOCO.

'What's that for?'

Rebus just winked, and the man pocketed the money, adding the word 'Cheers.'

'I always tip for service beyond the norm,' Rebus told Macrae. Nodding, Macrae dug into his own pocket and found a fiver for Rebus.

'Halfers,' the DCI said.

Steelforth was returning to the clearing. 'I need to get back to more important matters. When will you be finished here?'

'Half an hour,' one of the other SOCOs answered.

'Longer if need be,' Steelforth's nemesis added. 'A crime scene's a crime scene, no matter what other wee sideshows there are.' Like Rebus before him, he hadn't been slow to work out Steelforth's role.

The Special Branch man turned to Macrae. 'I'll inform ACC Finnigan, shall I? Let him know we have your full understanding and co-operation?'

'As you wish, sir.'

Steelforth's face softened a little. His hand made contact with Macrae's arm. 'I'm willing to bet you didn't see everything there is to see. When you're finished here, come back to Gleneagles. I'll give you the *proper* tour.'

Macrae melted; a kid on Christmas morning. But he recovered well, stiffening his spine.

'Thank you, Commander.'

'Call me David.'

Crouched as if for evidence-gathering some way behind Steelforth's back, the senior SOCO made a show of sticking a finger down his throat.

*

Three cars would be making their way separately to Edinburgh. Rebus shuddered to think what the ecologists would say to that. Macrae peeled off first, heading for Gleneagles. Rebus had driven past the hotel earlier. When you approached Auchterarder from Kinross, you saw the hotel and its grounds a long time before you reached the town. Thousands of acres, but few signs of security. He had caught just the one glimpse of fencing, alerted by a temporary structure which he took to be a watch-tower. Rebus shadowed Macrae on the way back, his boss sounding the horn as he turned into the hotel's driveway. Siobhan had guessed Perth as the quickest road, Rebus opting to retrace his cross-country route, pick up the M90 eventually. Still plenty of blue in the sky. Scottish summers were a blessing, a reward for the long winter's twilight. Rebus turned down the music and called Siobhan's mobile.

'Hands-free, I hope,' she told him.

'Don't be smart.'

'Otherwise you're setting a bad example.'

'First time for everything. What did you make of our friend from London?'

'Unlike you, I don't have those hang-ups.'

'What hang-ups?'

'With authority . . . with the English . . . with . . .' She paused. 'Want me to go on?'

'Last time I looked, I still outrank you.'

'So?'

'So I could cite you for insubordination.'

'And give the chiefs a good laugh?'

His silence conceded the point. Either she'd got lippier down the years, or he was getting rusty. Both, probably.

'Think we can talk the lab boffins into a Saturday shift?' he asked.

'Depends.'

'What about Ray Duff? One word from you and he'd do it.'

'And all I'd have to do in return is spend a whole day with him, touring in that smelly old car.'

'It's a design classic.'

'Something he won't begin to tire of telling me.'

'Rebuilt it from scratch . . .'

Her sigh was audible. 'What is it with Forensics? They all have these hobbies.'

'So you'll ask him?'

'I'll ask him. Are you carousing this evening?'

'Night shift.'

'Same day as a funeral?'

'Someone's got to do it.'

'I'm betting you insisted.'

He didn't answer, asked instead what her own plans were.

'Getting my head down. Want to be up bright and early for the march.'

'What have they got you doing?'

She laughed. 'I'm not working, John – I'm going because I want to.'

'Bloody hell.'

'You should come too.'

'Aye, right. That's going to make all the difference in the world. I'd rather stay at home to make my protest.'

'What protest?'

'Against Bob bloody Geldof.' She was laughing in his ear again. 'Because if as many turn up as he wants, it'll look like it's all down to him. Can't have that, Siobhan. Think about it before you sign your name to the cause.'

'I'm going, John. If nothing else, I need to look out for my mum and dad.'

'Your . . .?'

'They're up from London – and not because of anything Geldof said.'

'They're going on the march?'

'Yes.'

'Do I get to meet them?'

'No.'

'Why not?'

'Because you're just the sort of cop they're afraid I'll grow into.'

He was supposed to laugh at this, but knew she was only half joking.

'Fair point,' was all he said.

'Have you shaken off the boss?' A conscious change of subject.

'Left him at valet parking.'

'Don't joke – they actually have that at Gleneagles. Did he toot the horn at you?'

'What do you think?'

'I knew he would. This whole trip, it's shaken years off him.'

'Kept him out of the station, too.'

'So everybody wins.' She paused. 'You think you've got a crack at this, don't you?'

'What do you mean?'

'Cyril Colliar. The next week or so, nobody's going to be holding your leash.'

'I didn't realise I was up there in your estimation.'

'John, you're a year away from retirement. I know you want one last go at Cafferty . . .'

'And it seems I'm transparent, too.'

'Look, I'm just trying to –'

'I know, and I'm touched.'

'You really think Cafferty could be responsible?'

'If he's not, he'll want whoever was. Look, if it all gets a bit fraught with your parents . . .' Now who was changing the subject?

'Send me a text and we'll meet for a drink.'

'All right, I will. You can turn the Elbow CD up now.'

'Well spotted. Talk to you later.'

Rebus cut the connection; did as he was told.

Praise for THE NAMING OF THE DEAD

'Masterly . . . Ian Rankin's finest novel. It is more than a crime novel, or rather, Rankin's achievement is to show, convincingly, how crime permeates society'
Scotsman

'His richest and most complex work to date, it comes close to transcending genre fiction'
Scotland on Sunday

'Rebus may seem to be running on something very near empty, but there is no sign that Rankin has lost any of the energy to continue this consistently impressive series'
Sunday Times

'Combines the page-turning appeal of a modern police procedural with the moral complexity of a political novel'
Irish Times

'Politics crashes head on into Inspector Rebus's usual interests (solving grisly murders and supping pints) in the latest of this award-winning series. *The Naming of the Dead* set against the 2005 G8 Summit is yet another irresistible page-turner from the UK's best crime novelist'
Mail on Sunday

'Not only an intriguing murder-mystery but an excellent piece of reportage. Ian Rankin, despite his dodgy musical tastes, has produced yet another class act'
Evening Standard

'Classic Rankin, and if you're in love with the unchangeable Rebus, you'll relish it. It's page-turning, complicated crime'
Independent

'A big, sometimes elegiac, read'
Observer

'This is Rankin at his hard-bitten best'
Metro London

'This one, with its heady mix of crime and current affairs, is staggering. He is now at the top of his game and has almost catapulted himself out of the more limited crime genre altogether'
Daily Mail

'Rankin is on top form here, with a suitably scornful attitude to Bob Geldof and the wishy-washy Live 8 endeavour. Excellent stuff'
Dublin Evening Herald

'As much a political thriller as a crime mystery. His vivid descriptions of the so-called Battle of Princes Street are as good as any newspaper reports written at the time'
Glasgow Herald

'The plot is another Rankin corker, complex yet convincing, and played out on this occasion over only nine days against the backdrop of last year's G8 summit at Gleneagles, with its retinue of concerts and marches against poverty . . . The best crime novel you'll read this year'
Sunday Telegraph

'Rankin brings his characters to life with precision, and handles the novel's complex thematic relationships with his usual skill'
Times Literary Supplement